P9-CQM-791

My Congratulations to the
"Presents" Series and to its
Readers—
May the Romance live on!

With my very best wishes.
Penny Jordan

Dear Reader,

To me, Harlequin Presents® has always been at the cutting edge of contemporary romance and I've loved the uninhibited scope and pleasure of writing about today's relationships with their complex problems and passions.

Best of all, in these stories, the dream of love we nurse in our hearts can always be fulfilled. It's a special world we share—the magic of romance—and I hope you love it and enjoy it as much as I do, sharing the lives of others whose dearest wishes do come true.

Happy twenty-fifth birthday to Harlequin Presents!

Emma Darcy

EMMA DARCY
The Sheikh's Seduction

Harlequin Books

TORONTO • NEW YORK • LONDON
AMSTERDAM • PARIS • SYDNEY • HAMBURG
STOCKHOLM • ATHENS • TOKYO • MILAN
MADRID • WARSAW • BUDAPEST • AUCKLAND

ISBN 0-373-11953-4

THE SHEIKH'S SEDUCTION

First North American Publication 1998.

Printed in U.S.A.

CHAPTER ONE

"MY NAME is Sarah Hillyard. My father trains race-horses in Australia..."

The artless words of a twelve-year-old child.

A child he'd liked and remembered seven years later when he'd come to choosing a trainer in Australia.

Sheikh Tareq al-Khaima shook his head in self-derision. Stupid to have let a sentimental memory influence his judgment. He'd hired Drew Hillyard, entrusted him with the progeny of some of the best bloodlines in the world, and the man had proved to be a cheat and a crook, wasting what he'd been given in favour of sure money, bribe money.

It was an effort to remain civil, sitting beside him in the Members' Stand at Flemington Racecourse, waiting for the Melbourne Cup to be run. Recognised as one of the great races on the international calendar, The Cup was a prize coveted by trainers and owners. It made reputations. It sealed a horse's fame. It was the return on an investment.

If Firefly won today, Drew Hillyard might earn himself another chance. If Firefly lost, the trainer could kiss Tareq's string of thoroughbreds goodbye. The moment of truth was fast approaching. The horses were being boxed, ready for the start of the race.

"He should run well," Drew Hillyard said reassuringly.

Tareq turned to Sarah's father. The older man's brown

curly hair was streaked with lustreless grey and cut so short, the ringlets sat tightly against his scalp. His dark eyes were opaque, as though he'd fitted blinds over the windows of his soul. The memory of Drew Hillyard's daughter flashed into Tareq's mind—a glorious mop of burnished brown curls framing a fascinating face with eyes so dark and brilliant he'd loved watching them. He didn't want to even look at her father.

"Yes, he should," he answered, and returned his gaze to the track. Firefly had been bred from champion stayers. If he'd been trained properly he should eat this race. He *should*, but Tareq wasn't banking on it. None of the horses he'd placed in Drew Hillyard's stables had lived up to their breeding. The initial promise of the first two years had been whittled away by sly corruption.

Susan Hillyard claimed his attention. "Did you place a bet on Firefly, Tareq?"

He looked at her, wondering if she knew the truth. Drew Hillyard's wife—second wife—was a thin, nervous blonde. With every reason to be nervous, Tareq thought darkly. "I never bet, Mrs. Hillyard. It's performance that interests me. On every level. I like to see my horses fulfil the promise of their bloodlines."

"Oh!" she said and retreated, her hands twisting worriedly in her lap.

Sarah's stepmother.

My father's marrying again. Since my mother's made her home here in Ireland now, she's arranged for me to go to boarding school in England. So she can more easily visit me, she says. I get to go home to my father in the summer break.

A lonely, disillusioned child, her world torn apart by divorce. Tareq wondered what had become of her, where she was. Not here at Flemington. He'd looked for her, curious to see the woman she'd grown into. He was tempted to ask about her but revealing a personal interest went against his grain in this situation. Sarah, the child, was a piece of the past, eleven years gone. Comprehensively gone after today, if Firefly failed.

A roar went up from the crowd, signalling the start of the race. Tareq stood with the rest of the people around him, binoculars lifted to his eyes. The commentator's voice boomed over the loudspeakers, whipping up excitement. Tareq focused all his attention on the horse that had brought him here, a magnificent stallion who'd be worth his weight in gold if he won.

He was poetry in motion, well positioned for the early part of the race and running with a fluid grace and ease that was exciting to watch. He took the lead at the half-way mark and streaked ahead of the field. Too soon, Tareq thought. Yet he held a gap of three lengths into the last hundred metres. Then he visibly flagged, other horses catching him and sweeping past to the finishing post. Eighth. Respectable enough in a class field of twenty-two horses, people would say. Except Tareq knew better.

"Ran out of puff," Drew Hillyard said, his weather-beaten face appropriately mournful with disappointment.

"Yes, he did," Tareq coldly agreed, knowing full well that a properly trained champion stayer did not run out of puff.

"Want to accompany me down to talk to the jockey?"

"No. I'll have a word with you after the last race."

"Fine."

He and his wife left. Tareq was glad to see the back of them though he'd have to confront them later.

"Do you want me to do it?"

The quiet question came from his oldest friend, Peter Larsen. They'd been through Eton and Oxford together and understood each other as well as any two men could. It was Peter who had investigated Drew Hillyard's notable failure to make champions of champions. The paper evidence left no doubt as to the reason behind the obvious incompetence. To top it all, Drew Hillyard had even sacrificed a chance at the Melbourne Cup.

Tareq shook his head. Peter had saved him trouble on innumerable occasions but this wasn't usual business. "I was fool enough to choose him. He's mine, Peter."

A nod of understanding.

Drew Hillyard had broken a trust.

That was always personal.

CHAPTER TWO

SARAH helped her little half-sister to bed. Jessie had grown strong enough to move her legs herself but she was tired, her energy spent on all the anticipation, excitement and disappointments of the day. The latter had dragged her spirits right down and there was nothing Sarah could say to cheer her up.

Despite sitting glued to the television for hours before and after the running of the Melbourne Cup, Jessie hadn't seen the sheikh, whom she'd imagined in flowing white robes. Sarah had suggested he would probably be in a suit. Not a well-received comment. To Jessie's mind, a sheikh wasn't a sheikh unless he wore flowing white robes. Either way, the television had failed to put him on display.

And Firefly had lost. After looking as though he might take out The Cup for most of the race, the stallion had faltered with the finishing post in sight. A flood of tears from Jessie. She'd loved Firefly from the moment she'd first clapped eyes on the beautiful colt and she'd desperately wanted him to win.

"Mummy didn't call," she now grumbled, adding another disappointment to her list of woes.

Sarah tried to excuse the oversight. "It would be a busy day for her, Jessie, what with having to entertain the sheikh and everything. They've probably gone out somewhere."

Big blue eyes mournfully pleaded the injustice of it

all. "It's not fair. Daddy's had the sheikh's horses for four years and this is the first time he's come to Australia and I didn't even get to see him."

Neither did I, Sarah thought ruefully. Though it wasn't so important to her. Just curiosity to see what he looked like after all these years. Funny how some childhood memories remained vivid and others faded away. She'd never forgotten Tareq al-Khaima, nor his kindness to her over that first lonely Christmas in Ireland with her mother.

He'd been a young man then, immensely wealthy and strikingly handsome. Everyone at her mother's house parties had wanted to know him. Yet he'd noticed a forlorn child, eaten up with the misery of feeling like the leftover, unwanted baggage from her mother's first marriage, best out of sight and out of mind. He'd spent time with her, giving her a sense of being a person worth knowing. It was her only good memory from being twelve.

"Maybe there'll be a photograph of him in the newspaper tomorrow," she offered as consolation.

"I bet there isn't." Jessie stuck to gloom. "There hasn't been one all week."

Which had been surprising with the Spring Carnival in full swing and the social pages packed with photographs of visiting celebrities. Either the sheikh was not partying or he was camera-shy for some reason.

"And he's not coming to Werribee to see his other horses, either. Daddy told me he'd only be at Flemington."

"Well, the sheikh owns horses all around the world, Jessie." He'd been buying them in Ireland when she'd met him. "I don't suppose any particular string of them is special to him."

She wondered if he remembered her. Unlikely. Too brief a connection, too long ago. It was just one of those coincidences in life that Tareq's agent had assigned the sheikh's horses in Australia to her father to train. There'd been nothing personal in the deal.

"He came to see Firefly race," Jessie argued.

"That's because the Melbourne Cup is special." Having settled her half-sister comfortably, Sarah stroked the wispy fair hair away from the woeful little face and dropped a kiss on her forehead. "Never mind, love. I'm sure your mother will tell you all about the sheikh tomorrow."

Disgruntled mumbles.

Sarah ignored them as she made sure everything was right for Jessie; the electric wheelchair in the correct position for easy use when she needed to go to the bathroom, the night-light on, a glass of water on the moveable tray. It was amazing the amount of independence the little girl managed now. In fact, Sarah knew she really wasn't needed here at Werribee anymore. It was time to move on with her own life. Once the Spring Carnival was over, she would broach the matter with Susan.

Having completed her check list, Sarah moved to the door and switched off the overhead light. "Goodnight, Jessie," she said softly.

"Mummy didn't call and she promised she would."

The final petulant comment on a day that had not delivered its promises.

Sarah quietly closed the door on it, privately conceding Jessie had cause to feel let down. Her mother should have called. That had been a real promise, not a wish or a hope. Real promises should be kept.

Sarah grimaced at the thought as she moved along the hall to the twins' room. It was so hopelessly idealist in this day and age where keeping promises was a matter of convenience. Wasn't her whole life an illustration of not being able to count on them? It was about time she accepted the real world.

She looked in at the boys. Her seven-year-old half-brothers were fast asleep. They looked as innocent as babes, mischief and mayhem cloaked with peaceful repose. The problem with children was they were innocent. They believed in promises. When disillusionment came it hurt. It hurt very badly.

Mummy didn't call…

The words jogged memories of another Melbourne Cup day. She'd been ten, the same age as Jessie, and left behind at Werribee in the care of the foreman's wife. *Her* mother hadn't called, either. She'd been too busy with Michael Kearney, planning to leave her husband and daughter and go off to Ireland with the promise of becoming the fourth wife of one of the wealthiest men in the horse world.

Her mother had made good on *that* promise, and when Michael Kearney had chosen wife number five, the divorce settlement had been astronomical. It had certainly helped make the ex-Mrs. Kearney an attractive proposition to an English Lord. Sarah could safely say her mother had never looked back after leaving Werribee. She'd been appalled when her daughter had rejected "the chances" lined up for her, returning to Australia to help with Jessie.

Sarah didn't regret her decision. It was strange how

far away that life in England seemed now. The question was…where to go from here? She wandered into the living room, curled up on the sofa and gave the matter serious consideration.

She'd always loved books. They'd been her escape from loneliness, her friends and companions, doors that opened other worlds for her. She'd had her mind set on getting into some career in publishing. Maybe her degree in English Literature would still hold her in good stead there, though she had no work experience and probably openings at publishing houses were few and far between. Still there was no harm in looking for a position.

Melbourne? Sydney? London?

She instinctively shied from going back to England.

A new life, she thought, one she would make on her own. Though how best to do it kept her mind going around. When the telephone rang it startled her out of a deep reverie. She leapt to pick up the receiver, glancing at her watch simultaneously. Close to nine-thirty.

"The Hillyard Homestead," she rattled out.

"Sarah… I promised to call Jessie. Is she still waiting?"

Susan's voice was strained. She didn't sound herself at all. But at least she hadn't forgotten her daughter. "No, she was tired," Sarah answered. "I put her to bed at eight. Do you want me to see if she's awake?"

"No, I… I just thought of it and…oh, Sarah…" She burst into tears.

"Susan, what's wrong?"

Deep, shuddering breaths. "I'm sorry…"

"It's okay. Take it easy," Sarah soothed, trying to contain her own fast-rising anxiety. "Try to tell me what's happened.'' Please, God! Not another dreadful accident!

"The sheikh...he's taking all his horses away from your father.''

"Why?'' It made no sense. Unless... "Surely not because Firefly didn't win the cup?''

"No. There's...there's more. The past two years...but you know what they've been like, Sarah. It was hard for Drew to keep his mind on the job.''

What was she justifying? Had her father mismanaged the training?

"It'll ruin us,'' Susan went on, her voice a wail of despair. "It'll make other owners uneasy. You know reputation is everything in this business.''

"I don't understand.'' She'd been too busy with Jessie to take an active interest in what was happening with the thoroughbreds in her father's stables. "What is the sheikh's complaint?''

"It's all about...about performance.'' She broke into tears again.

"Susan, put Dad on. Let me talk to him,'' Sarah urged.

"He's...he's drinking. There's nothing we can do. Nothing...''

Not if you're drunk. Sarah bit back the retort, knowing it was useless. All the same, her father's growing habit of hitting the bottle could be at the root of this problem. It was all very well to seek relief from stress but not if it led to shirking responsibilities.

"Tell Jessie I'll call her tomorrow.''

The phone went dead.

No point in holding the receiver. She put it down. The living room suddenly felt cold. If her father was ruined, if that sent him further along the path of drinking himself into oblivion...what would happen to his and Susan's marriage? What would happen to the children? It was always the innocent ones who were overlooked.

Sarah shivered.

Did Tareq al-Khaima realise what effect today's decision would have? Did he care? How bad was the situation?

Sarah shook her head helplessly. She had no idea to what extent her father had failed in giving the sheikh satisfaction.

But she did know the circumstances behind his failure.

Tareq had been sympathetic to her once. If he remembered her...if she could get him to listen...

It was worth a try.

He was staying at the Como Hotel. She remembered her father mentioning it. If she went there as early as possible tomorrow morning...

Anything was worth a try to stave off disaster.

CHAPTER THREE

SARAH glanced anxiously at her watch. The drive into
the city had taken over two hours. The morning was
slipping away from her. It was almost eight o'clock and
she was still locked in Melbourne traffic. A sleepless
night and a heavy weight of worry wasn't doing much
for her judgment on which were the faster transit lanes,
either.

She'd left Werribee as early as she could but not as
early as she would have liked. It had taken time to in-
struct one of the stable hands in the house routine so he
could look after the children until the foreman's wife
could come. It wasn't the best arrangement but this was
an emergency situation.

Her main fear was the possibility she was already too
late to make any difference to Tareq's decision. He may
have acted yesterday, lining up another trainer to take
his horses. Or he could be at Flemington right now, discussing business. The Spring Carnival wasn't over yet.
It was Oaks Day tomorrow. Many owners gathered with
trainers at the racetrack at dawn each morning, watching
the form of favoured horses.

On top of which, even if Tareq was at his hotel, there
was no guarantee he would see her. Or talk to her. Let
alone listen to what she had to say. All Sarah could do
was hope and pray for a chance to change his mind
before his decision became irreversible.

When she finally reached the Como Hotel, she did a

double take. Despite its being in South Yarra, outside the main city area, she had expected a big, plush, ostentatiously luxurious establishment, the kind of place one automatically associated with oil-wealthy sheikhs. The Como was relatively small, almost boutique size. Sarah hoped it meant Tareq was more approachable.

She found a parking station just off Chapel Street, left the jeep there, and walked back to the hotel.

The moment she entered it, the decor screamed class—quiet, exclusive class—marble floors, black leather sofas, floral arrangements worthy of being called exquisite modern art. It might not be ostentatious luxury but it was just as intimidating to anyone who didn't belong to the privileged people.

Sarah could feel herself bridling against its effect and mentally adopted a shield of untouchability to carry her through gaining entry to Tareq's presence. She knew from experience with her mother's high-strata world that her appearance would not be a critical factor. The dark brown corduroy jeans and fawn skivvy would pass muster anywhere these days. The wind had undoubtedly tossed her unruly curls but that didn't matter. Neither did the fact she wore no make-up. "Being natural" could be just as fashionable as designer clothes.

The concierge directed her to the reception area, around to the left and down a flight of steps, privacy from the street effectively established. One elegant free-standing desk was apparently enough to serve the guests. The woman behind it smiled invitingly. Sarah willed her to be obliging, too.

"I've come to call on Sheikh Tareq al-Khaima. Is he in?"

"Yes, Ma'am. Whom should I say is calling?"

"If you'll just give me his suite number..."

"I'm sorry, ma'am. That's against our security rules. I can call up to his suite for you. What name should I give?"

Security. Of course. This place was probably as tight as Fort Knox—no unwanted visitors allowed past the steel doors of the elevator. "Sarah Hillyard," she stated flatly, resigning herself to the inevitable. If Tareq didn't want to see her, she couldn't force him to.

Her nerves knotted as the call was made and the message passed on. There seemed to be a long hesitation before an answer was given. Sarah's tension eased slightly when the receptionist smiled at her, indicating no problem.

"He's sending Mr. Larsen down to fetch you. It should only be a minute or two, Miss Hillyard."

"Fetch me?"

"There's a special key for the executive floor. The elevator won't take you up without it."

"Oh! Thank you."

Relief poured through her. Past the first hurdle. Though Mr. Larsen, whoever he was, might prove to be another barrier. She wondered how big Tareq's entourage was. He wouldn't have come alone to Australia and might well have taken over the whole hotel. Such information hadn't been of interest to her until now and it was too late to ask her father or Susan for more facts.

When the steel doors opened, a tall, fair-haired man, impeccably dressed in a silver-grey suit, emerged from the elevator. His face was thin and austere; high cheekbones, long nose, small mouth, and very light eyes. He looked to be in his early thirties and carried an air of lofty authority. He inspected Sarah as though measuring an adversary; a swift, acute appraisal that left her highly rattled.

One eyebrow was slightly raised. "Miss Hillyard?"

"Yes. Mr. Larsen?"

He gave a slight nod and waved her into the elevator. No smile. His eyes were a silver grey like his suit. Very cold. He didn't speak as he used a key to set the compartment in motion, nor did he acknowledge her in any way as they rode upwards. Sarah felt comprehensively shut out from this man's consciousness.

Fighting another rise of tension, she inquired, "Have you been with Sheikh Tareq al-Khaima for a long time, Mr. Larsen?"

He looked directly at her, his mouth curling slightly. "You could say that."

Oxford accent. Upper-class English. "Are you a friend or do you work for the sheikh?" she asked, needing to place him.

"I'm his trouble-shooter. Are you trouble, Miss Hillyard?"

A hatchet man, she thought. "Am I seeing him or you?"

"The sheikh will see you personally."

The man's superior manner provoked her. "Then I hope I'm trouble, Mr. Larsen."

"Brave words, Miss Hillyard."

And probably foolish. Getting anyone close to Tareq offside was hardly good politics.

Mr. Larsen turned away, though not before Sarah saw a flicker of amusement in the light grey eyes. A chill ran down her spine. This man's amusement would undoubtedly be aroused by the anticipation of seeing someone cut to pieces. It did not augur well for her meeting with

Tareq. But at least she was seeing him, which gave her a chance at persuasion.

Sarah clung to that reassurance. The elevator stopped. Mr. Larsen led her along a corridor, stopping at a door on which he knocked before using a key to open it. Poker-faced once more, he ushered Sarah into a suite full of light.

The blinds had been lifted from two huge picture windows, allowing a spectacular view over the city. Tareq stood at the window. Although his back was turned to her and he was anonymously clothed in a navy blue suit, Sarah had no doubt who it was. The thick black hair, dark olive skin, his height and build, brought an instant wave of familiarity, despite the passage of years between their meetings. Yet Sarah was just as instantly aware of something different.

She remembered him as carrying an air of easy self-assurance, confident of who he was and what he wanted from life. To a child who felt no security about anything, it had seemed quite wonderful to be like that. Now she sensed something more, a dominant authority that didn't bend.

Perhaps it was in the square set of his shoulders, the straightness of his back, the quality of stillness telegraphing not only total command of himself, but command of the situation. Even the plain dark suit implied he needed no trappings to impress himself on anyone. He didn't have to do anything. He certainly didn't have to turn to her need to appeal to him.

Her formidable escort had followed her into the suite and shut the door behind them. He waited, as she did, for Tareq to acknowledge their presence. Waiting for the entertainment to begin, Sarah thought, and wondered if she should take the initiative and greet Tareq. The silence seemed to hum with negative vibrations, choking off any facile words.

"Did your father send you, Sarah?"

The quiet question had a hard edge to it. Without moving, without so much as a glance at her, Tareq had spoken, and Sarah suddenly realised he was standing in judgment. She sensed his back would remain turned to her if her answer complied with whatever dark train of thought was in his mind. She didn't know what he expected to hear. The truth was all she could offer.

"No. It was my own idea to come to you. If you remember, we met in Ireland when…"

"I remember. Did your father agree to your coming here?"

Sarah took a deep breath. Tareq al-Khaima was not about to be swayed by reminiscences. He was directing this encounter and she had no choice but to toe his line.

"I haven't even spoken to my father. Nor seen him," she answered. "I was at Werribee yesterday, looking after the children. Susan, his wife, phoned last night. She was terribly distressed…"

"So you've come to intercede for him," he cut in, unsoftened.

"For all of them, Tareq. It doesn't just affect my father."

"What do you intend to offer me to balance what he's done?"

"Offer?" The concept hadn't occurred to her. No way could she compensate for whatever had been lost. 'I…I'm sorry. I have no means to pay you back for…for my father's mismanagement."

"Mismanagement!"

Her heart leapt as he swung around. The vivid blue blaze of his eyes shot electric tingles through her brain, paralysing her thought processes. Her whole body felt caught in a magnetic field. Her stomach contracted. Goose bumps broke out on her skin. She couldn't even breathe. Never in her life had she felt such power coming from anyone. She was helpless to do anything but stare back at him. His gaze literally transfixed her.

The initial bolts of anger transmuted into laser beams. It felt as though he was peeling back the years, remembering how she'd been at twelve, then piling them on again, rebuilding the woman she was now, studying her, seeing if she measured up to whatever he thought she should be.

Sarah struggled to reclaim her mind. He had changed. The shock of such blue eyes—an inherited gene from his English mother—against his dark complexion still held fascination but she saw no kindness in them, nothing to encourage hope. His strikingly handsome face had matured into harder, sharper lines, his softer youthfulness discarded. She knew him to be thirty-four, yet he had the look of a man who wielded power at any level and commanded respect for it. He was armoured, in every sense.

His mouth suddenly curved in a half-smile. "How can dark chocolate shine so brightly?"

They were the teasing words he'd used about her eyes the morning he'd invited her to ride with him on her stepfather's estate in Ireland, she on a pony, he on a thoroughbred stallion. Sarah floundered in a wash of memories. She had no reply to the remark, any more than she'd had then.

"You haven't learnt any artifice, Sarah?" he asked.

The abrupt change to a more personal line of conversation confused her. "I don't know what you mean."

The half-smile took on a cynical twist. "You're a grown woman, yet I still see the child. The same rioting brown curls. The same appealing face, bare of make-up. Clothes that are nothing more than clothes. Perhaps that was intentional. Artifice in lack of artifice."

She blushed at his dissection of her appearance and hated herself for letting him make her feel gauche. "Look! This isn't about me," she implored.

"The messenger always carries many messages," he stated, his eyes mocking her assertion. "You're a beautiful young woman. Beautiful women usually know and use their power."

His gaze dropped to her breasts, making Sarah acutely conscious of the stretch fabric of her skivvy hugging their fullness. Then he seemed to mentally measure her waist, the wide leather belt she wore undoubtedly aiding his calculation. The curve of her hips and the length of her legs were inspected, as well, much to Sarah's growing embarrassment.

His appraisal of her feminine *power* increased her awareness of the strong sexual charisma which, at twelve, she'd been too young to recognise in him. It was certainly affecting her now, so much so it prompted the realisation he was probably used to women throwing themselves at him. Wealth alone was considered an aphrodisiac. With his looks...

An awful thought occurred to her. When Tareq had asked what she intended to offer him, had he imagined a proposition involving sexual favours? Was he summing up her desirability in case she took that line of persuasion?

Sarah almost died of mortification. She wouldn't even know how to go about it. Men hadn't featured largely in her life, none in any intimate sense. As for Tareq...she was losing all her bearings with him.

"The question is...how grown up are you?" he mused, the glitter of speculation in his eyes discomforting Sarah even further.

"I'm twenty-three," she replied, fervently wishing everything could be more normal between them. She remembered feeling safe with Tareq all those years ago. She didn't feel safe now.

"I know how old you are, Sarah. Your age doesn't answer my questions."

"I told you...this isn't about me."

"Yes, it is. It's very much about you. How long have you been at Werribee?"

Was this a chance to start explaining? "Two years," she answered, and it was as though she'd slapped him in the face.

She physically felt his withdrawal from her. There was the merest flicker in his eyes, a barely visible tightening of his jawline, no other outward sign. He remained absolutely still, yet she felt every thread of connection with her being ruthlessly cut.

"So...you've been assisting your father," he said coldly.

Sarah realised he'd just cloaked her with her father's sins, whatever they were. "Not with the horses. I've had nothing to do with them," she rushed out. "I've been helping with Jessie. She's ten years old, Tareq. My little half-sister. And she's a paraplegic."

A muscle in his cheek contracted.

Sarah plunged on, wanting him to understand the

background. "Two years ago, Susan was terribly ill, being treated for breast cancer. Then Jessie was injured and Susan couldn't cope. There were the boys, too…"

"Boys?"

"My half-brothers. Twins. They're seven now but they were only five when I came back to Werribee to help."

"You were asked to do so?"

"No. Susan wrote about Jessie."

"Where were you then?"

"London. I'd just finished my finals at university."

"And you dropped everything to help them?"

He made it sound incredibly self-sacrificing but it wasn't. "I've always loved Jessie. How could I not come when she had to face never walking again?"

He frowned. "You stayed with her…all this time."

"I was needed." It was the simple truth.

His eyes bored into hers and she felt the reconnection. It was a weird sensation, as sharp and quick as a switch being thrown, making her nerves leap and jangle, an invasion she had no control over.

"The child belongs to its mother, Sarah," he said quietly. "She is not the answer to your loneliness."

Her heart pumped a tide of heat up her neck and into her cheeks; burning, humiliating heat. He knew too much about her. He was plucking at her most vulnerable chords. It *had* felt good to be needed. And wanted.

Her reluctance to cut herself off from those feelings had influenced her choice to stay in her father's home longer than was strictly necessary, but she did realise it was time to move on. Though this latest disaster confused the issue.

"I can't desert them now. Don't you see?" she

pleaded. "My father will be ruined if you take your horses away. What will happen to the children?"

"It is not your responsibility," he retorted harshly. "Your father brought this outcome upon himself."

"Did he? Did he?" she cried, and plunged into a passionate defence. "Was it his fault his wife got cancer? Was it his fault Jessie was crippled? There were astronomical medical bills and the house had to be renovated to accommodate a handicapped child, a special suite built on with all the aids for Jessie to learn to be independent, a special van bought to transport her. There were so many adjustments to be made, and the continual cost of physiotherapy, masseurs... Do you wonder that my father was distracted from doing his job properly?"

Sarah was out of breath from the frantic outpouring of words. Her eyes clung to Tareq's, begging understanding. If he could see through her so easily, couldn't he see this, too?

Or did he see an ongoing problem?

"But things are better now," she hastily declared. "Susan's been cleared of the cancer. She's fine. No trace of secondaries. And Jessie has made fantastic progress. It's amazing how much she's learnt to do for herself. The boys have become good at helping her, too. So you see...my father no longer has so many worries on his mind. He could concentrate on the training if you'll just give him another chance."

Her plea seemed to be falling on deaf ears. There was no visible reaction to it on Tareq's face, no trace of sympathy. She needed some response, some hint of whether he was reconsidering his stance or not.

His brick wall silence tore at her nerves. It went on for an agonising length of time. Sarah fought against a mounting sense of defeat. Was there anything more she could say that might touch him?

"Leave us, Peter."

The quiet command startled her into jerking her head around. She'd forgotten the presence of Mr. Larsen behind her. He was still there, a witness to everything that had been said. His gaze was locked on Tareq, the chilling light eyes slightly narrowed, as though trying to discern the reason behind the command, or perhaps sending a silent warning that a witness was a wise precaution against trouble.

Whatever he thought, he left without a word, not even glancing at Sarah. The door clicked shut after him, emphasising the continued silence and making Sarah intensely aware she was alone with Tareq. She spun her attention back to him, fighting a rush of inner agitation. Her heart beat chaotically as he started walking towards her.

"You fight very eloquently on your father's behalf," he said, though he didn't look impressed. "I find that quite remarkable since he didn't fight for you. He gave you up, freeing himself to marry again without any encumbrances and have this family you care so much about."

"Whatever my father's shortcomings, the children are innocent," she argued, inwardly quailing as Tareq came closer and closer. "It's more for their sake that I'm asking you to reconsider your decision."

He stopped so close she had to tilt her head back to look up at him. His eyes burned into hers with mesmerising intensity. "And if I don't reconsider, you are willing to give them more devoted service. More of your time," he said, stroking her cheek with feather-light fingertips as though seeking to get under her skin and feel all she was.

Sarah's legs turned to jelly. His nearness was over-powering, his touch insidiously weakening both her mind and body. She'd never experienced anything like it in her life. Movement was beyond her. She could hardly think.

He raked back some curls and tucked them behind her ear, his eyes simmering into hers, holding them captive to his will. "I like your giving heart, Sarah. It's a rare thing in today's world."

She swallowed hard, trying to rid herself of the constriction in her throat. "Can't you give, too, Tareq?"

"Perhaps."

"You were once kind to me," she pleaded.

"And I'll be kind to you again, though you may not appreciate the form it comes in."

"What do you mean?"

"A bargain, Sarah. You want me to give your father another chance. I want something in return."

She literally quaked. He was still fiddling with her hair, winding curls around his fingers, tying her to him. It took all her willpower to force out the words, "What is it you want?"

"For the length of time it takes for your father to prove he can be trusted to do his best by my horses, you will stay with me. Let us say...you will be a hostage to his conscientious efforts to redeem himself."

Dear God! He did mean to tie her to him! Sarah tried to rally her wits out of their state of shock. "You mean...like a prisoner."

"No need to be so grim. You can be my travelling companion...my social secretary..."

Euphemisms for current mistress? Or was her imagination running riot, along with her hormones?

"Staying with me should not be a hardship," he assured her. "I'll pay you a generous salary for your devoted service."

"Like what?" Sarah's mind was spinning, unable to decide what was real or unreal. How *devoted* was the service to be?

"What did your father pay you for all the hours you gave to his family?"

She flushed. "It's my family, too."

"Two years of unpaid labour, Sarah? Two years of putting your life on hold with nothing to show at the end of it?"

"Is there a price on love, Tareq?"

"Oh, yes." A taunting twist of his mouth mocked her naivety. "There's always a price. You've been paying it. And you'd pay more. So make up your mind as to where it's best paid, Sarah. You continue to give yourself to your family with potential ruin on their doorstep, or you give yourself to me, securing the second chance you've been pleading for."

"Why does it have to be this way?" she cried. Why did he want her with him?

"It's a question of trust," he answered, a relentless beat in his voice. "I don't trust your father. He betrayed the confidence I placed in him. If you trust him to come good on another chance, you have nothing to fear from this bargain and a lot to gain."

That was the crux of it. Testing her trust in the trust she was asking him to give. She saw the hard ruthlessness in his eyes and knew there was no mercy in him.

If he didn't get the performance he wanted, he would extract compensation, one way or another.

Her mind was in chaos. What if her father didn't pull himself together and apply himself to fulfilling Tareq's expectations? On the other hand, having stared ruin in the face, surely the prospect of being handed another chance would sober him up. Sarah didn't—couldn't—place much store in his caring for what might happen to her, but his love for his other children had always been much in evidence.

And the plain truth was, they didn't need her so much as they needed each other. She'd only ever been an extra, waiting in the wings to be called on. Now that Jessie was capable of managing herself, there was no real reason to stay. The best she could do for them was to give them the chance Tareq was offering.

His hand slid from her hair and travelled around her jawline to cup her chin. "Tit for tat, Sarah. I risk my horses. You risk yourself. Is it a deal?"

A two-way gamble. Put like that, his proposition was understandable. Reasonable. But it was difficult to hang on to reason, swamped as she was by the sexual current coursing from the touch of his hand, sensitising her skin and making a mash of her insides. She didn't feel safe with him.

Yet without him, Jessie and the twins wouldn't be safe. Innocent victims. As she had been. Sarah couldn't let that happen. She stared into the diamond-hard blue eyes of Tareq al-Khaima and willed him to be honourable.

"All right. I'll do it," she said decisively.

The flash of satisfaction she saw curled her stomach.

Could she trust him to keep his word?
There was no guarantee.
Only risk.

CHAPTER FOUR

TAREQ was not slow in acting on Sarah's decision. There was no time given for second thoughts. He moved straight to the telephone, leaving Sarah to listen as he set up his side of the bargain.

"Peter, call Drew Hillyard. Tell him his daughter, Sarah, is here with me. Due to her special pleading, I am inclined to change my decision and leave my horses with him."

This apparently evoked some expostulation from his trouble-shooter. Whatever was said made no difference to Tareq. He calmly resumed speaking.

"I'm sure you'll think of a way to put an effective stop to that. Just get Hillyard here, Peter. As soon as possible. We'll hear him out first, then move to break the link. From both sides."

Another pause. Sarah wondered what link they were talking about.

"Sarah has agreed to act as surety. She'll be coming with me when I fly out tonight. You'll have to stay behind and wrap this up, Peter."

Tonight! Sarah moved shakily to an armchair and sat down, dizzied by the speed at which her life was about to change. She stared out the window at the view of the city. Where would she be this time tomorrow?

"Tell Hillyard to bring his wife with him. Best to get everything settled in one hit."

The receiver clicked down.

"Sarah, have you eaten anything this morning?"

She turned blankly to the man who would direct everything she did from now on. He frowned at her, picked up the telephone again and proceeded to order a selection of croissants, muffins, and a platter of cheese and fruit. Having finished with room service, he considered her thoughtfully.

"You're not going faint on me, are you, Sarah?" he asked. "You've stood up bravely so far."

Brave words, Miss Hillyard… She wondered what Peter Larsen thought of her now. Trouble. Definitely trouble. For some reason the thought gave her satisfaction.

A spark of pride made her answer, "I'm not getting cold feet if that's what's worrying you."

"Good!" He moved purposefully to the kitchenette beyond the dining suite. "Coffee or tea?"

Surprised at his intention to serve her, she asked, "Shouldn't I be doing that?"

He laughed, a soft ripple of private amusement. "I'm being kind. Which do you prefer?"

No point in arguing. "Coffee, thank you. With milk."

She watched him make it and bring it to her, noting he seemed more relaxed. Her own tension had eased, whether from the release of having carried through her purpose, or from the weird sense of having her fate taken out of her hands, she didn't know. Maybe she was suffering some aftermath from the shock of hard decision-making. Whatever the reason, she felt oddly detached, even when Tareq came close, placing her coffee on the low table in front of her and settling on the sofa nearby.

"You said we'd be flying out tonight. Where are we

going?'' she asked, trying to get some bearings on what would be her new life.

"The U.S."

She'd never been there. It might have been an exciting prospect under normal circumstances, but she seemed to be anaesthetised to all feeling at the moment. Shock, she decided. She'd been bombarded by the unexpected and driven to accept it. Recovery time was obviously needed.

She sipped her coffee. Tareq watched her, not with the high-powered intensity she had found so disturbing. It was more a clinical observation. It didn't touch her inner self. Since he appeared disposed to answer questions, she tried to think of what she needed to ask.

"Will I get to say goodbye to the children?" Already they seemed distant to her. It was as though she had stepped from one world into another.

"Yes," he assured her. "All going well at the meeting with your father, you and I will proceed to Werribee."

"I drove here in a jeep," she remembered.

"Your stepmother can drive it home. You will come with me in my car. There'll be time for you to pack your belongings and take your leave of Jessie and the twins."

"While you wait for me."

"Yes."

A hostage isn't allowed to roam free, she thought. I'm tied to him. So why aren't I feeling a sense of bondage?

Because it doesn't feel real. Not even this conversation seems real. Sooner or later reality will kick in again and then I'll feel it. In the meantime, talking filled the emptiness.

"Jessie wants to meet you," she prattled on. Strange irony. Was Tareq a benefactor or a curse? "She watched for you yesterday, hoping to see you featured on television, but you weren't. She was very disappointed.''

"Then I'll make up for the disappointment by meeting her this afternoon," he said smoothly.

"You've got the wrong clothes on," she told him. "A sheikh is supposed to wear sheikh clothes."

He smiled. "I'm afraid I don't have them with me. Will the person do?"

The smile made him even more magnetically handsome. "I'm sure Jessie will be impressed." As she herself had been at twelve...impressed and flattered to be given his attention. Perhaps he was always kind to children. They made it easy. They didn't question so much.

Her mind flitted forward, away from the past and on to the future. "I guess I'm to have Peter Larsen's ticket on the plane tonight."

He shook his head. "There are no tickets, Sarah. I have my own plane."

Of course. A private luxury jet, no doubt. She was moving up in the world. Like her mother. Only to a higher strata again. That should amuse her but it didn't. "Will we be accompanied by many people?"

"I prefer to travel lightly. Only Peter came with me on this trip."

Which meant she would be alone on the plane with Tareq. Though not quite alone. There would have to be a pilot, a steward, perhaps a co-pilot for such a long flight. Whatever...there would be no getting lost in a crowd. Was she to be his closest associate?

"Peter Larsen implied he'd known you a long time."

"Since school days at Eton."

So Mr. Larsen was very upper-class English. Sarah

wondered if he knew her second stepfather. "I presume you trust him," she said a little cynically.

"Yes. He's never given me reason not to."

A question of trust...

"How long do you expect it to take...for my father to prove himself to you?"

He eyed her speculatively. "Did you watch the running of the Melbourne Cup yesterday, Sarah?"

"Yes. On television."

"Then you must have seen with your own eyes that Firefly did not run the distance he should have been trained for."

She frowned, remembering how the horse had tired. "I thought the jockey had misjudged his run."

"No, it was more than that. The horse wasn't up to the distance and he should have been."

Firefly...

A suspicion wormed into Sarah's mind.

Jessie still loved the horse...but what did her father feel about it?

"I'll have Firefly entered in the Melbourne Cup next year," Tareq went on. "If he runs as well as he should..."

"You can't expect him to win!" Sarah cried in alarm, a rush of agitation smashing the odd numbness that had claimed her. "No one can guarantee a winner in the Melbourne Cup. The favourites hardly ever win."

"I agree," Tareq answered calmly. "As long as it's a fine effort for the distance I'll be satisfied."

A year of her life. Then her fate—the fate of her family—hung on Firefly's performance. Dear God! She had to talk to her father, make sure he understood. If he had some prejudice against the horse, he had to bury it or they would never get to the other side of this bargain.

A knock on the door.

Tareq rose to answer it. The timing was fortunate. Sarah struggled to contain a surge of panic. She had to remain calm, confident. Tareq was far too perceptive. He would pounce on any hint of a problem with Firefly, and if he pursued the truth and found out what had been hushed up, he might decide he had no grounds for even the tenuous trust Sarah had pleaded for.

It was room service arriving. The ordered food was set out on the coffee table. Tareq tipped the waiter and saw him out. "Try to eat, Sarah. We have a long day ahead of us," came the sensible advice.

She had absolutely no appetite. Her stomach was in turmoil. Nevertheless, eating precluded any dangerous conversation so she started with the fruit which was relatively easy to slide down her throat. Melon, strawberries, fresh pineapple...she picked and nibbled, using up time.

Satisfied she was well occupied, Tareq moved back to the telephone on the desk and made a series of calls. Sarah didn't listen to what was spoken. Her thoughts were too loud, clamouring over each other. What if she didn't get the opportunity to be alone with her father? Would Tareq tell him what the test of his training was to be?

Suddenly there were many ifs and buts. Sarah fretted over them until it struck her that her father might actually prefer to be rid of Tareq's horses, however crazy it was in a professional sense. Although he had held on to them after Jessie's accident, being paid for their training, he might have had no heart in their doing well. Maybe even taking some dark satisfaction out of making sure they didn't.

Yet surely that was at odds with a trainer's character...the drive to win, to get the best results, to chalk up enviable records. On the other hand, it could explain her father's drinking bouts. She had put them down to stress, though perhaps she had mistaken the cause of stress...a mind divided against itself.

It seemed stupid to have had Firefly not running the distance, with his owner—a man as astute and as knowledgeable about horses as Tareq—watching his failure to perform. Yet...weren't there people who wanted to be caught, wanted whatever they were doing to end?

She should have waited to discuss the issue with her father. She should have...

Her heart jumped at another knock on the door.

Her father?

She leapt to her feet, spinning around to face...Peter Larsen...as Tareq admitted him to the suite. The two men stood murmuring to each other. With a muddle of anxiety running rampant in Sarah, the question shot from her lips.

"Did my father agree to the meeting?"

It startled both men into turning to her. Her heart kicked into a gallop. She concentrated on Peter Larsen. He was responsible for making the arrangements. His sharply inquisitive gaze told her nothing. He seemed more interested in pegging her into a newly revised slot than answering her question.

"Why wouldn't he agree, Sarah?"

It was Tareq who spoke, drawing her attention to him, and once again the power of the man came at her full bore, his eyes like electric probes, making her whole body quiver inside. How was she going to cope with this man when he could affect her like this? He'd caught her so off-guard she was hopelessly stumped for an answer. Her frantic mind finally seized on one.

"Pride. You fired him yesterday. He might be angry about me interceding on his business. I didn't think about him so much as…"

"He's here. In Peter's suite," Tareq stated, removing her uncertainty. His face took on a ruthless cast as he added, "If he doesn't agree to my terms, I'll be a very surprised man. Don't concern yourself with contingency plans, Sarah."

He was set on the bargain. He wanted it to happen. He would *make* it happen. She could see it in his eyes. And she had the prickly feeling it had nothing to do with horses anymore. It had to do with her.

"Tell the Hillyards I'm on my way, Peter," he said, nodding to the man who needed no other signal to do the sheikh's bidding. "Sarah, it's best you wait here while we settle this business with your father."

She tore her gaze from him and stared at the door closing behind Peter Larsen, wanting to snatch him back, wanting the orders altered.

"Have you changed your mind?" Tareq asked quietly.

She flashed him an anguished look. "I want to be in on the discussion with my father. I might have done wrong…"

"Then it's up to him to say so. You have done your part. The choice is now his."

Cool, clear reason. Yet she sensed the fire of purpose in Tareq and knew instinctively it wouldn't be deterred by anything. Tentacles of fear started weaving through her, clutching at her heart and mind. What had she set in motion? Where would it end?

"Speak now if you prefer not to go through with this, Sarah. I won't take it kindly if you try to back out after I've made a settlement with your father."

She took a deep, deep breath.

The equation was the same.

The future security of the children was at stake.

"As you said, it's up to my father. If he agrees, my agreement stands."

Again the flash of satisfaction in his eyes, curling her stomach.

"This may take some time. Please be at ease here. Use whatever facilities you like. Treat the suite as your own."

He left her to stew over what was transpiring between the two parties.

It was over an hour before he came back, an hour of agitated pacing, of sick turmoil, of swinging through so many emotions, Sarah felt like a limp rag when he re-entered the suite. She could tell nothing from his expression. It was guarded, controlled, yet he carried an aura of success.

"Well?" she challenged, on painful tenterhooks as to the outcome.

"I believe we've come to a clear and mutual understanding. Your father will continue training my horses. He and your stepmother would like to speak to you, Sarah. If you'll come now..."

It was done.

Really done.

The next year of her life belonged to Tareq al-Khaima. He might not be dressed in traditional clothes but Sarah had no doubt he was a sheikh through and through, born to rule, used to dictating his own terms, determined that his will be carried out.

The only question left was…what was his will where she was concerned? Her soul trembled at the thought of finding out that reality.

CHAPTER FIVE

THE stretch limousine heightened Sarah's awareness of what life with Tareq was going to be like. She sat beside him on a lushly cushioned, blue velvet seat, every luxury at hand—cocktail bar, television, radio, telephone—and tinted windows around them, forming a cocoon of privacy from the ordinary world. Even the chauffeur, having been given directions to the Hillyard farm at Werribee, was removed from them by a glass partition.

Tareq dominated her space, dominated her thoughts, dominated her every sense.

Her gaze was pulled again and again to the hands resting on his thighs; long-fingered, brown-skinned, elegantly formed yet suggesting a tensile strength capable of catching and holding anything they wanted to. The future of her family was in those hands now, and she was within very personal reach of them any time he chose to make physical contact.

Her nostrils kept picking up the subtle scent of some male cologne. She hadn't noticed it in the hotel but in the close confines of the car, it intruded enough for her to try to define it, thinking it might define the man. Like the navy suit he wore, it was classy, understated, yet tantalising in suggesting something primitive overlaid with especially tailored sophistication.

Her ears were constantly alert for any movement from him, a shift towards her, a recomposure of himself. He seemed to have mastered the art of utter stillness, which

42

made Sarah extremely conscious of her own little outbreaks of nervous fidgeting.

He hadn't touched her since he'd drawn her into consenting to the bargain. He didn't need to. He knew she was now tied to him by honour and integrity. She could feel his touch on her heart and mind and soul.

In her mouth was the sweet-bitter taste of what he had drawn from her father on her behalf, whether by threat or persuasion or simple instruction, she didn't know. Susan's tearful gratitude she could accept as a natural response, but her father's halting speech had been a raw exposure of hidden hurts, intensely embarrassing.

It had touched on feelings they had never talked about, never acknowledged, and because nothing of that ilk had ever been said between them before, Sarah had difficulty in deciphering what was sincere or simply forced out of the situation. She couldn't help thinking of the Christmas in Ireland where she'd spilled too much to Tareq...a kind stranger she'd never expected to meet again...a man who was acutely, dangerously perceptive.

"Did you tell my father to say those things to me?" she blurted out, wanting to know how pervasive Tareq's influence had been in that last painful scene at the hotel.

Out of the corner of her eyes she saw his head turn towards her. Sarah had to summon up her courage to look directly at him, needing to maintain a protective shield around herself while she held his gaze.

"What things, Sarah?" he asked, the powerful blue eyes scanning for cracks in her hastily erected defences.

"About not letting me down again."

"You think he didn't carry any guilt over abandoning you to your mother's whims when you were twelve?"

"Did you make him feel guilty, Tareq?"

A slight shrug. "Perhaps I tapped at his conscience in explaining why you felt you could approach me personally...the past connection between us."

"You must have laid it on thick," she accused.

He was completely unabashed. "Sometimes it's very beneficial, very sobering, for people to be faced with the consequences of the decisions they make."

There was a hard glint of ruthlessness in his eyes.

Her father had certainly been sobered up by the time she'd walked into Peter Larsen's suite. His alcoholic bender the night before had left him looking drawn and haggard, his eyes red-rimmed, but he'd spoken with convincing determination about making good on this second chance. Having accepted Tareq's terms, whatever they were, he could hardly do anything else. He'd undoubtedly been made to face that his career in training was on the line.

It was the second part of his speech she questioned. He'd moved straight on to expressing—openly expressing—his regret in failing her as a father; his realisation that he'd selfishly accepted her ongoing assistance to his family, thinking only of their need instead of seeing she was putting her own life on hold; his hope that her new position with Tareq al-Khaima would be a door to a lot of opportunities for her; and finally, his fervent vow to live up to her good faith in him and be there for her if she ever called him in need.

They had to be lines fed to him by Tareq. Under duress. Although it was possible her father had taken them to heart. Either way, it was too late for a real rapprochement between them. Tareq was taking her away.

"I didn't have much evidence of his caring for you, Sarah," Tareq remarked, reading her thoughts with disquietening ease. His mouth quirked. "And what good is a hostage without a strong value of caring? I thought it worthwhile to add an appropriate load of guilt."

Questions answered.

Sickened by his logic even as she recognised its truth, Sarah dropped her gaze and turned her face to the side window. They were out of the city and travelling through the countryside to the place she thought of as home. Except it had ceased being her home eleven years ago when her status had changed to occasional visitor. More recently she'd been the live-in family help. But she didn't belong there. She didn't belong anywhere.

Which had probably made it easy for Tareq to claim her with no one to protest, no one to fight for her. She was on her own. But that didn't mean she was a push-over for anything he wanted. Her hands curled into determined fists. If he made unreasonable demands on her she would fight him.

Without looking at him, she asked, "What are the duties of a travelling companion?"

"To travel with me." His tone was lightly amused.

Her nails dug into her palms. "Nothing else?"

"Oh, I daresay we'll come to various little accommodations."

"Like what?"

"You can unclench your hands. I've never taken an unwilling woman to bed with me."

Smarting at his knowingness, she flashed him a furious glance. "It's all very well for you, sitting in your control box."

He laughed, his eyes dancing, teasing, enjoying his control. "Are you a virgin, Sarah?"

"That's none of your business!" she cried, futilely willing the rush of hot blood to her face to recede.

"Just curious. You're so uptight…"

"There've been plenty of men interested in me."

"Was the interest returned?"

She thought of the "precious" young men her mother had lined up as "catches" for her before she'd left London. Compared to Tareq al-Khaima they were bloodless boys. She was swimming with a shark in these waters. Which raised the question of how many *willing* women he'd gobbled up along the way.

"Let's talk about you," she said defiantly.

"By all means. What do you want to know?"

"No doubt you've had quite a love-life."

"A little correction there. I don't think love has ever entered into it. Desire, certainly. Satisfaction, yes. Mutual pleasure definitely attained…"

"All right!" she cut him off, disturbed by the images running through her mind. "Let's say sex-life."

"Ah, yes. Well, I can't deny having had considerable experience."

The smile lurking on his mouth was tauntingly sensual. Sarah could feel her blood heating up again. She had no difficulty in believing he was a very sexy man when he put his mind to it. If he put his mind to it with her…but it would be madness to succumb even if she did wonder what it might be like with him. Where could it lead? He was a sheikh, tied to a culture that was very foreign to her.

"Won't it put other women off, having me tagging along with you everywhere?" she commented archly, wondering if he'd looked down the track to see the consequences of *his* decision.

"Not at all. You'd be surprised," he said cynically.

He was right. Even marriages didn't stop some people from going after what they wanted.

"What about your family? It could give them the wrong impression."

His mouth curled with some private satisfaction. "They will think what I tell them to think. Where my family is concerned, it suits me very well to have you with me, Sarah."

His ruthless streak was showing again. This time it piqued her curiosity. "Why?" she asked, wondering if he was at odds with them.

He weighed the question, his eyes regarding her speculatively. Eventually he said, "My background is similar to yours…a broken marriage, my mother returning to England, the agreement that I be educated there at Eton and Oxford. It got me out of the way for my father's second wife and the family they had together."

No wonder he had been sympathetic to the child she had been, cut adrift between two worlds and not really belonging to either. He really had understood and possibly empathised with her sense of apartness, her loneliness, the feeling of being a shuttlecock in an adult game that sought only personal gratification.

"The difference is…the complication is…I'm my father's eldest son, despite my mixed heritage," he said sardonically. "The sheikhdom had to pass to me when he died."

"Did you want it?"

A flash of ruthless possessiveness in his eyes. "I was entitled to it."

And no one was going to take *that* away from him, Sarah interpreted.

"Though the truth is…I am not in tune with my people. For years now, my uncle has ruled in my absence while I maintain a diplomatic role. It has suited us both very well. But circumstances change. My oldest half-brother will soon marry the daughter of a very powerful family. Ahmed and Aisha make a formidable coupling. If they work against me, it could stir some political instability. My uncle is pressing for me to marry a woman of his choice to cement my position."

Sarah inwardly recoiled against the concept of an arranged marriage although she knew it was done and accepted in eastern cultures. For Tareq, it would seem the most sensible decision to make.

"You don't want that?" she queried.

A flash of steely pride. "No one dictates my life anymore, Sarah."

She could well believe it!

"Naturally I will be attending my half-brother's wedding. And you'll be with me. It neatly disposes of any machinations my uncle might have in mind."

So Tareq had a purpose for her. Sarah could see it was very convenient for him to have a woman on tap who'd agreed to stay with him for a year. No possibility of a refusal to accompany him. No running away, no matter how sticky the situation.

The bargain he'd offered her suited him on many levels.

"I suppose you'll want us to pretend to be…" *lovers* teetered on her tongue and she quickly withdrew it as a possibly dangerous suggestion. "…closer than we really are in front of your family."

Amusement sparkled. "I don't think any pretence will be necessary."

Did he mean to seduce her before then? Sarah's heart flipped over. Her whole body started churning as she remembered how he'd measured her desirability. Then, when he'd offered the bargain, she'd stood like a mesmerised idiot, letting him touch her. Had that assured him he could make her *willing*?

"You'll soon get bored with me, you know," she fired at him, hating the thought he was confident of arranging everything his way. She might have agreed to being his companion but she wasn't his slave!

His amusement broke into a laugh that tap-danced all over Sarah's nervous system. "I can't remember when I've felt so challenged by a woman. But you could be right. A year is a good test."

A year...

God help her!

She turned to look out the window again, knowing more now but not exactly comforted by the knowledge. They were passing by familiar Werribee landmarks. Soon she would be saying goodbye to all this, leaving the safe little world where she had been closeted for two years.

Her heart began to ache. She would miss Jessie and the boys. Though Tareq was right. They were Susan's children, not hers. All the same, it didn't mean she couldn't love them...her half-sister and half-brothers. They were the only family she had.

Tareq had capitalised on her feeling for them.

She was risking herself for their sake and they'd probably never know. Not that it mattered. She knew. Regardless of what happened to her, something good had been achieved. Jessie and the twins would not become the flotsam of a broken family.

Like her.

Like Tareq.

Except no one in their right mind could think of Tareq al-Khaima as *flotsam*.

CHAPTER SIX

As THE limousine came to a halt in front of the house, Sarah saw Jessie zoom along the veranda in her electric wheelchair, heading for the series of ramps that would bring her down to the road. She could go almost anywhere on the property in the custom-made chair, the powered base giving it a four-wheel suspension and amazing mobility. The novelty of seeing a stretch limousine at close quarters was not about to be missed.

Jessie wasn't the only one whose curiosity and interest were aroused. The foreman's wife came to the veranda railing, watching as the chauffeur opened the passenger door. Sarah waved to her as she stepped out, determined on acting as naturally as possible in the circumstances. The startled look at Sarah's arriving in such style turned to awed wonder as Tareq emerged from the car.

"Sarah!"

Jessie's cry of surprise claimed attention. The little girl was also staring goggle-eyed at Tareq, the chair halted several metres away as she took in the man accompanying her older half-sister.

Sarah was momentarily tongue-tied, not having prepared what to say to Jessie. Tareq had dominated her thoughts during the trip here. Now the moment was upon her, she instinctively seized his arm and drew him forward with her. Since this was his doing, let him handle it.

"Jessie, remember how disappointed you were not

seeing the sheikh yesterday? Well, here he is… Sheikh Tareq al-Khaima!''

"Really?'' Incredulity was almost instantly mixed with excitement and pleasure, lighting up her face and dismissing all her woes. "You came out to see me?''

"Sarah told me about you, Jessie,'' he answered, smiling indulgently and offering his hand. "You'll have to forgive the suit. I don't wear robes outside my own country.''

"Oh!'' Jessie blushed. Her small hand was gently enfolded in his. "That's all right. You look…well, sort of like a royal prince anyway,'' she said in an admiring rush. "And the car is fantastic!''

"Would you like to see inside?'' Tareq invited.

"I'd love to!''

Sarah realised she was still hanging on to Tareq's arm. She quickly released it as they moved to make room for Jessie to manoeuvre her chair into position beside the car. It was crazy to have seized on closeness to him for some kind of reassurance. Yet he was good with Jessie. Faith…if it could be called that…in his kindness to children had been justified.

"That's a great machine you're driving,'' he remarked, watching her zip the chair around the passenger door which he'd opened for her viewing.

"It's the Rollerchair Trail Blazer,'' she proudly informed him.

He grinned. "Well, I'd have to say it blazes, Jessie.''

She laughed. "You mean the colours. Dad got them specially for me. I reckoned with a red seat and a yellow frame, everyone would see me coming.''

"Couldn't miss,'' he agreed. "It's a brilliant combination. I'm afraid this car is fairly dull in comparison.''

"No, it's not," Jessie insisted, peering in at the plush interior.

"Would you like to have a ride in it with me? I could lift you in and strap you up and sit beside you, showing you everything while the chauffeur drives us around."

"Yes, please," Jessie cried, thrilled at the prospect. "Wait till I tell the twins about this!" she crowed at Sarah.

Her arms went trustingly around Tareq's neck as he gently scooped her out of the electric chair, no hesitation at all, despite his being a virtual stranger. Somehow his innate strength of personality and self-assurance evoked confidence in him. Sarah, too, had accepted his trustworthiness when she'd been a child. She wished it could be the same now.

"Sarah, will you move my chair out of the way, please?"

She operated the toggle switch with the ease of long practice, reversing the chair to a safe distance. Jessie had no compunction in instructing Tareq how best to settle her on the seat of the car and he showed no discomfort with her disability, chatting away naturally while he settled her as promised.

"Perhaps you'd let the lady on the veranda know what Jessie and I are doing," he said to Sarah as he straightened up, hard blue eyes turning the request into a command.

Only then did she begin to understand there was purpose in his kindness. They'd come to collect her passport and possessions, and he was diverting Jessie while the real business was done. "Of course," she answered, forcing a smile. "Enjoy the ride, Jessie."

"Aren't you coming, too?" came the slightly plaintive plea.

Tareq answered for her. "Sarah has other things to attend to, Jessie. She'll be busy for a while. I was hoping, after our drive, you'll show me what you've got in the special rooms your father had built for you. If there's anything more like your Trail Blazer..."

Jessie giggled. "It's the best. But there is some other clever stuff I can show you."

A master manipulator, Sarah thought, as she left them to head up to the house. Though it had to be conceded he was making the situation less harrowing for her, keeping Jessie happily occupied and probably setting up an understanding of why Sarah would be going with him instead of staying at the farm.

The foreman's wife stood at the top of the steps to the veranda, her gaze darting between Sarah and the limousine. Ellie Walsh and her husband had been working for the Hillyards since Sarah was a child. Ellie was in her forties, a tall spare woman with a no-nonsense attitude. She invariably wore a shirt and jeans and kept her hair cut in a short, boyish style. Practicality was her byword.

"What's going on?" she asked as Sarah started up the steps.

The limousine was moving off. Sarah smiled to relieve any worry. "Jessie has just made the acquaintance of Sheikh Tareq al-Khaima. He's treating her to a bit of high life in his car."

"The sheikh!" Shock and alarm crossed Ellie's face. "Has he come about his horses?"

It was obvious she knew the training wasn't up to par.

Probably everyone who worked here knew but none of them wanted to be unemployed.

"Everything's all right, Ellie." Sarah could only hope it would be. "The sheikh has offered me a position and I'm taking it. I'm here to pack and say goodbye."

Ellie was dumbfounded, her fears about the future frozen in the face of such unexpected news.

"Susan is on her way home. She's got the jeep and will be collecting the boys from school," Sarah went on. "I really appreciate your minding Jessie at such short notice today…"

"No problem," Ellie muttered. "You're really going with the sheikh, Sarah?"

"Yes. It's an opportunity to widen my horizons again."

Ellie shook her head, still stunned at the turn of events. "The children will miss you."

"I'll miss them, too, but…" She shrugged. "…I can't stay here forever."

"I guess not," came the weak rejoinder. "Well, I'll leave you to it. I wish you luck, Sarah." She gave a funny laugh. "Mind you don't end up in a harem."

It was a possibility for the duration of the brother's wedding, Sarah thought ironically, though she had the strong impression Tareq didn't hold much with tradition. In any event, taking a wife was not on his agenda. Squashing the issue of marriage was.

Having seen Ellie on her way, she went into the house to set about uprooting herself again. It was difficult to keep depression at bay as she dragged her million-miler suitcase out of the storage cupboard and set it on her bed, ready for another packing, another move. She'd made a personal home of the room Susan had given her and it hurt to look at one more part of her life which was now over.

Her gaze mournfully skimmed the colourful collection of soft toys she'd knitted while sitting with Jessie. They were lined up on top of her chest of drawers, waiting to go to the boys' school fete. A stack of library books was on her bedside table, some of them destined to be left unread. Photographs depicting Jessie's progress were glue-tacked to the frame of the mirror on her dressing table. No point in taking them. They belonged here.

Sarah fiercely concentrated on what had to be taken...clothes, toiletries, important documents. The sooner her packing was accomplished, the better, she told herself, and set about tackling her clothes first. Most of them were leftovers from her student days, hardly a suitable wardrobe for the high life, but Sarah shrugged off that problem. If Tareq wanted her dressed differently he could pay for it. She hadn't exactly applied for the position of his companion.

A shiver of trepidation ran down her spine. Would he think he was buying her if she let him pay for clothes? He obviously didn't have any high expectations of women, viewing those who'd been in his life as nothing more than sexual partners. *Willing* sexual partners. When he'd said he'd never felt so challenged by a woman, did he mean because she wasn't offering herself to him?

Sarah shook her head, trying to dismiss the rising anxieties. Stupid to keep worrying about the future. The decision was made. Whatever the outcome of a year with Tareq, she had to take it in her stride and let it flow past her. It was one thing she used to be good at, letting things flow past her.

It had been different with Jessie and the twins. Her

involvement with them had been so easy, natural…an uncomplicated love, given and returned. Sarah hoped it would always be the same with them. All going well, they would still be here next year when she returned with Tareq for the Melbourne Cup.

Her packing was well under way by the time Jessie returned with Tareq. She stood still, listening to the high excited voice leading her important visitor down the hall to her especially equipped domain. There was no pause outside Sarah's door. Jessie had to be still in ignorance of her half-sister's imminent departure.

Almost an hour later, Sarah took her luggage out to the veranda. The chauffeur collected it and stowed it in the limousine. Susan and the boys still hadn't arrived. Sarah waited outside until she caught sight of the jeep approaching the gate into the property, then steeling herself for the inevitable leave-taking, she walked quickly into the house and straight to Jessie's suite.

A swell of emotion broke past her guard as she knocked on the door. Tears stung her eyes and her chest was so tight, the deep breaths she forced herself to take were painful. Keep it bright, keep it simple, and make it quick, her mind dictated. It would be easier that way, easier for everybody. Having blinked back the tears, she pasted a smile on her face and opened the door.

Why her gaze went first to Tareq, she didn't know. It was Jessie she had to face, yet somehow he dominated even this parting scene…sitting in the chair she usually sat in, commanding attention simply by being in this room. He looked at ease, yet she felt the driving force behind his kindly facade and her heart quailed at what she had invited upon herself in accepting his bargain.

The electric chair hummed into life. Sarah tore her

gaze from Tareq and looked anxiously at Jessie, now turning away from the desk where she'd obviously been showing Tareq some of her sketches. She had a real gift for drawing, a talent Sarah had encouraged her to develop since it was not dependent on two active legs. One day it might lead her into a rewarding and fulfilling career.

"You can sit on my bed, Sarah," she invited, her little face still glowing with excitement. "Are you all packed, ready to go with Tareq?"

The knowledge and the ready acceptance in the question jolted Sarah. "I...yes. The chauffeur put my luggage in the car," she answered weakly, searching for and finding no sign of distress in the child. "I know it's sudden, Jessie, but..."

"Oh, you couldn't miss out, Sarah," came the eager urging. "You'll have a wonderful time with Tareq."

"You don't mind my going?" It amazed her, disturbed her that Jessie seemed to care so little about losing her.

"Gosh, Sarah! It's not as if everybody's sister gets asked to travel with a sheikh." She looked absolutely entranced with the idea. "You're so lucky!"

"Yes, aren't I?" she agreed, trying to inject some enthusiasm into her voice.

She darted a glance at Tareq as she sat on the bed, wondering if he'd brainwashed Jessie into thinking he was sweeping Sarah off on a magic carpet. The look he returned telegraphed very clearly he left nothing to chance when he wanted his purpose achieved. Sarah knew she should feel grateful he'd removed any trauma from the situation. Instead, she felt cheated, as though he'd wiped out the value of her involvement with her family.

"I'll be thinking of you all the time," Jessie went on. "Promise you'll send me postcards of wherever you go, Sarah?"

"Of course I will." Her inner stress eased a little at this evidence of wanting a continuing connection.

"I'm going to get a big map of the world and put it on my wall. Every time I get a postcard from you, I'll stick in a pin of where you are so I'll only have to look at it to know and think of you there. Isn't that a good idea?"

One of *his*? "I'll be thinking of you, too, Jessie. I hope you'll write to me."

"I'll write you very special letters, Sarah."

This declaration was accompanied by a secretive smile which she shared with Tareq. His smile in response indicated a conspiratorial arrangement. Sarah hoped Tareq wouldn't conveniently forget his part of it once they were away from here. She didn't want Jessie disillusioned by broken promises. On the other hand, she couldn't argue with the ideas he'd implanted. It seemed he had gone out of his way to ensure she remained a presence in her family, however far away she was.

"I'll look forward to hearing all your news, Jessie," Sarah said in warm encouragement. "You must write me news of the boys, too."

She giggled, delighted with the plans concocted with Tareq. "It's going to be such fun!"

The eruption of noise in the house heralded the twins' approach. They burst into Jessie's room, two hyperactive bundles of trouble with wild, curly hair and big brown eyes, determined on finding the sheikh and seeing him for themselves. Jessie performed the introductions and both boys looked their fill of the man, somewhat daunted by his powerful presence.

"Mum said you're taking Sarah with you," Tim spoke up, showing his misgivings about this arrangement.

"Sarah is ours," Tom stated belligerently.

"Sarah will always be yours," Tareq answered, smiling his assurance. "She's your sister and she loves you. Coming with me won't make any difference to how she feels about her family."

"But I don't want her to go away."

"Don't be a baby, Tom," Jessie cried in exasperation. "Sarah's a grown-up and she hasn't had any time for grown-up things with us. You've got to be fair."

Another one of Tareq's ideas?

"Do you want to go, Sarah?" Tim asked.

"I do need to do something more with my life, Tim," she answered, "though I've loved being here with you."

"Who's going to tell us bedtime stories?" Tom demanded.

"I will," Susan said from the doorway. "And I think you should thank Sarah for giving you so much of her time instead of making her feel bad about leaving you."

"We didn't mean to make you feel bad, Sarah," Tim rushed out. "We want you to be happy."

"Well, she'll be real happy with Tareq," Jessie declared, giving her younger brothers a supremely smug look. "*I* went for a ride in the stretch limousine!"

The boys instantly set up a clamour to be taken for a ride, too. Tareq good-humouredly agreed, inviting Jessie to lead them out to the car. She had a lovely time, playing Queen Bee, escorted by the sheikh who had apparently taken on the guise of fairy godfather.

"Will you be happy with him, Sarah?" Susan asked, scanning her anxiously as they trailed after the limousine party.

"I expect it will be an experience," she returned dryly.

Susan shook her head fretfully. "You've done so much for us. I don't know what to say...except thank you."

"Try to keep Dad off the bottle, Susan."

"I think Tareq has taken care of that. Your father got caught up in doing things he really hated and now he'll be free of it, thank God!"

The passionate relief in Susan's voice piqued Sarah's curiosity. She stopped walking and stayed her stepmother from following the others off the veranda. "I'm not sure I understand," she said, her eyes sharply questioning.

Susan looked intensely discomfited. "Never mind. Better that you don't. Drew needs to save some pride. He feels bad enough it was you who got Tareq to give him a fresh start. He won't let you down on this, Sarah."

"It's not just me. It's the family," Sarah retorted, frustrated by Susan's evasion. There were some things more important than pride and she tried to press them home, given this was her last opportunity to do so. "I'd hate to see you and Dad break up."

She shook her head. "I'd never leave your father. We've been through so much. He stood by me when I was hopelessly incapacitated. I'd stand by him through anything, Sarah. Don't worry about us. We'll get over this hump and turn it all around."

Faced with such faith and determination, Sarah didn't have the heart to question further. Marriage was a private business to the two people involved and nothing she said would make any difference anyway. It certainly hadn't in the past.

They remained on the veranda, watching Tareq directing the final show for the day. The limousine took off for another spin around the property, carrying three exuberant children and the man who held all their lives in his controlling hands for the next, testing year.

"I'm sorry you were so messed around by the divorce, Sarah," Susan said, apparently stirred into an awareness of where her stepdaughter was coming from in the previous conversation.

"Not your fault," Sarah replied dismissively. Sympathy had not been around when she'd needed it and hindsight sympathy only made the omission worse.

"I could have offered to keep you here with us. But I didn't," came the regretful admission.

Sarah had had a gutful of guilt from her father. She didn't want it from Susan, too. "Water under the bridge," she said curtly.

"I want you to know you'll always be welcome here. Any time. For as long as you want."

Too late, Sarah thought with rueful irony. A debt was owed now. People were uncomfortable with debts. It colored the flow of natural feelings. Though not with the children. They would never know. Nevertheless, it would lie between her and their parents, denying her the closeness she would have liked.

"Thank you," she said, acknowledging the offer which had been sincerely made, however unlikely it was to be taken up. Tareq was about to dominate her life for the next twelve months. Perhaps longer if…her heart clenched with a sense of ominous urgency as she turned to her stepmother. She'd almost forgotten the most critical thing of all!

"Please tell Dad to do his best with Firefly, Susan. It's important. Tell him from me it's terribly important if he doesn't want to let me down."

Tareq might have freed her father from his self-made stress, but Firely's performance was her passport to freedom.

"I'll tell him," Susan replied.

"You won't forget?" Sarah pressed.

"I promise."

Promises...she'd had a gutful of them, too...broken ones.

The limousine came back.

Her time here was up.

The children were happy to say goodbye...hugs and kisses and well wishes. Sarah settled on the plush seat beside Tareq. The chauffeur closed the door, the last separating act. She watched her family waving her off as the limousine moved away from them. There was no point in her waving. They couldn't see her. She was behind tinted windows, cut off from them, enclosed in Tareq's world.

"Thank you for making it easy," she said stiffly.

"Was it easy?"

She grimaced, her eyes drawn to his by the gentle probe for honesty. "Yes and no."

He nodded, understanding her ambivalence. There was both comfort and disquiet in his understanding so much. Recalling his skill at manipulating everyone today, Sarah was goaded into making one stand on principle.

"I appreciate your...graciousness...in the circumstances. But if you've made promises to Jessie, please keep them, Tareq."

The blue eyes held hers, unperturbed, unwavering. "I never make promises I don't intend to keep."

Sarah suddenly felt foolish for raising the matter. Everything he'd said today indicated he set a lot of store by trust. In his life it was probably as precious a commodity as it was in hers.

"Then you *will* let me go if Firefly runs well next year," she said, wanting him to voice that promise in undeniable terms.

She felt the power behind his eyes intensify, boring into her, flooding her veins with tingling heat, enmeshing her mind with threads of entanglement that would never let go unless he willed it.

"You will be freed...from being a hostage."

His words rang hollowly in her ears, rendered meaningless by vibrations of a much more personal connection. Sarah knew in her bones she would never be free of Tareq, even given the lifting of the hostage tie, even given he didn't want her with him beyond that time.

The impression he'd left on her twelve-year-old mind was still with her, and that had only been a week of her life. How much stronger would it be after twelve months?

"Why are you doing this to me?" It was a cry of protest, wrung from the depths of her being.

He didn't question it. He didn't pretend he didn't know what she meant. "You think you don't touch me, Sarah? What am I doing here?" His eyes glittered with a reckless pleasure in the challenge. "We shall travel this road together until I know all of it."

CHAPTER SEVEN

SARAH didn't want to get out of bed. The moment she woke she remembered what was ahead of her today—the trip to Silver Springs, being at Tareq's side amongst other people—and the now familiar tightening of nerves around her stomach made her feel sick.

Ten days she'd been with him—another three hundred and fifty-five to go—and at this rate of personal upheaval, she was not going to survive the distance. It was difficult enough, coping with the tension of her position when she and Tareq were alone together. The thought of others looking on, questioning the relationship, speculating, as they surely would, stirred an intense inner violence. She wanted to hit out at something but there was nothing to hit out at, nothing of any substance.

Tareq could not have been more gentlemanly towards her, more considerate. There was no physical touching she could object to, no unseemly words she could hang him on. It was the constant waiting and expectation of something more to come from him that had her on edge.

Worse was her growing obsession with the man, the insidious attraction she couldn't control, the tug-of-war between denial and desire, the awful, vulnerable sense of being powerless to stop what was happening to her.

Unless she reneged on their bargain and left him.

Which was impossible.

She'd given her word. And Tareq was ruthless enough to withdraw the agreement with her father if she failed

65

to keep it. There was no escape and he knew it. He had all the time in the world to make his move on her. If he chose to.

We shall travel this road together until I know all of it.

With those relentless words beating through her mind, Sarah turned over, punching her pillow for the lack of anything else to punch. Her gaze fell on the lush tropical garden in the courtyard beyond the double glass doors of her bedroom. She'd forgotten to pull the curtains last night. Not that it mattered. The guest suite she'd been given was completely private, even to the courtyard outside. She couldn't accuse Tareq of intruding on this space, yet the knowledge it was his house and he was in it with her, was constantly intrusive.

This past week on the west coast of Florida should have been heaven, a vacation in a warm sunny climate, one of the most handsome and wealthiest men in the world intent on giving her pleasure, making no demands on her whatsoever except to relax and enjoy herself. It had turned into a hell of ever-increasing awareness. Of him. Of herself.

Her mind flitted over the procession of events, tracing the progress of her torment. The plane trip to the States hadn't been too bad. Perhaps emotional and physical exhaustion had drawn a protective curtain around her. Tareq had been solicitous of her comfort, coaxing her to eat and drink at various intervals during the flight, but she'd managed to put him at a distance from her, sleeping a lot, watching videos, reading magazines. He'd let her be, not pushing his company on her.

After they'd landed at Fort Myers, she'd focused on external things, looking at where they were going, asking questions about what they were passing. They'd driven through a fabulous estate development comprising dozens of magnificent homes and luxurious condominiums set on perfectly landscaped and beautifully maintained lawns and lakes and gardens, three golf courses, neighbourhood pools and gyms and tennis courts, a private beach and marina facing onto the Gulf of Mexico. It had surprised her to learn it was one of Tareq's property investments, another mind-boggling sample of the wealth at his disposal.

"Have you come to check on it?" Sarah had asked.

"Not particularly. I kept one of the houses facing the beach for myself. It's a convenient base for this time of year. People come to spend the winter months here."

Only very rich people, the kind who mixed in his league.

"And it's not far from Ocala. Handy for looking at the horses on the ranches around there. I've been advised there's a couple of yearlings that might interest me."

"So we're here on business."

"A short vacation first." Blue eyes smiling warm kindness. "You need it."

Kindness with a purpose...always a purpose behind everything Tareq did.

The first day...arriving at this fantastic house with its impact of glorious space; huge airy rooms, tall ceilings, lots of glass, the decor in all shades of sea colours; pale blues and greens, white tiles on the floor, rugs patterned with sea-shells, wicker furniture...a beach house, but on such a luxurious scale it seemed a misnomer to Sarah. Being given her own suite and meeting the couple who took care of everything—Rita and Sam Bates—created a comfort zone. For the first day.

The second day had actually been fun, bicycling around the estate, trying out the pool and hot tub, discovering the wonderful taste of stone crabs, a special delicacy of the area served by Rita that night. Seeing Tareq stripped to a minimal swimming costume had been slightly unnerving but not overly disturbing. She could still concentrate on other things at that point.

The third day he'd taken her on an exhilarating airboat ride over the Everglades, skimming the seemingly endless grassy marshes, seeing the fascinating bird life and alligators, amazingly a nest of baby ones. She had enjoyed it, though she'd become very conscious of Tareq watching her enjoyment, gleaning some private pleasure in it.

She had the sense he had forgotten what uncomplicated joy was like and was relearning it from her. It had made her feel good, useful, of some positive value, giving him something that had been lost from his life.

The next day there'd been a rapid escalation of good feelings. Too rapid. It reminded her of sugar candy being spun around a stick. One was so entranced with the fairy floss, the stick supporting it was lost in a cloud of pink.

Tareq had taken her to Smallwood's Store and she'd wandered around the historic trading post, fascinated by all the relics of the past which had once been sold to the pioneers of the Everglades, coming in their boats which they tied to the piers of the old wooden structure at waterside. Furs and plumes were traded here for food and cloth and all manner of household goods from lamps to treadle sewing machines, medicine, books, every kind of working tool. The place was a treasure chest of past lives and Sarah revelled in the experience of stepping back in time.

Tareq had seen it all before but he wasn't bored, wasn't the least bit impatient with her journey of discovery. He shared the knowledge he'd picked up from reading local books, fed her interest, indulged her fascination, and watched her with a warmth that kept getting under Sarah's skin.

There was something very intoxicating about approval. She'd had so little of it in her life. Yet she found herself wary of its bestowal from Tareq, not quite trusting it, looking for the purpose behind it. Was Tareq subtly plumbing her unfulfilled needs and wants to establish a deeper tie with him?

I don't think any pretence will be necessary.

Better if the woman he used for confronting his uncle was very convincingly stuck on him.

The fifth day they'd spent on the beach. The sand was gritty with broken-up shells. They lay on loungers shaded by umbrellas, swam in the relatively warm waters of the gulf, picnicked from a hamper Rita had prepared for them. It should have been a blissfully relaxing day, if only Sarah had been able to keep her eyes off Tareq.

She couldn't help it. In clothes the man was strikingly handsome. Virtually naked, for hours on end, lying beside her, walking in and out of the water, towelling himself, his physical beauty was almost mesmerisingly addictive, compelling her gaze to linger on his perfectly proportioned and powerfully muscled body. More disquietening was the desire to touch. His skin gleamed like rich, bronze satin and it was a continual strain to clamp down on the impulse to reach out and graze her fingers over it.

He caught her watching him slap oil around the calves

of his long, strong legs. "Want some?" The blue eyes twinkled teasingly, knowingly, shaming her with the realisation he had to be aware of his effect on the opposite sex and she was proving no different from any other woman.

"No. I'm fine, thank you," she'd answered stiffly.

He'd returned to his task, smiling to himself, and there was still a little curve on his lips when he lay back down on the lounger, his eyes closed to her. Was he amused that she couldn't stop herself from being attracted to him? Satisfied it was beyond her control? Or was she being hopelessly neurotic, reading a connection to her into a smile which might simply be expressing gratification in a lazy, sensuous day.

Sarah's gaze slid down over his taut stomach and fastened on the very male bulge at his crotch. She felt a point of sexual heat start burning between her own thighs and quickly turned away from him, squirming both physically and mentally from the wild desire to know what he was like as a lover, to feel that body intimately engaged with hers. She'd never actually lusted over a man before. It made her uncomfortably conscious of her own body, as well as his.

On the sixth day they'd gone fishing with Captain Bob, which had been another new and exciting experience until she'd had the misfortune to hook a very big fish on her line. She wasn't strong enough or practised enough to reel it in. Tareq had stood behind her, his arms around her waist, one hand helping to hold the rod in its holster, the other closed over hers on the handle of the reel, showing her how to play the fish on the line.

It wasn't a sexual embrace, merely a supportive one, yet it blew away all Sarah's concentration on what she was supposed to be doing. It was Tareq who eventually landed the fish. All she remembered was his breath warming her ear as he gave instructions, the strength of his fingers pressing on hers, the electric excitement coursing through her body from the contact with his, the sudden scorching hunger to feel everything he could make her feel.

When he moved away, admiring the catch netted by Captain Bob, Sarah was left trembling violently, shocked by the snaking intensity of sexual need which was still writhing through her. She dropped shakily onto the closest bench seat and stared at the fish, caught no matter how much it struggled. Like her, she thought, only Tareq was still playing her on his line.

"Let it go," she'd croaked, then fiercely challenged the quizzical look from Tareq. "I want it released."

"Your fish," he conceded, nodding to Captain Bob.

It wasn't really hers. He'd caught it. Perhaps that was why she felt such a savage surge of satisfaction, watching it swim free again, a silver flash in the water, escaping the painful confusion of being pulled into a different, alien world.

On the seventh day, Tareq had casually announced he was taking her shopping for clothes.

Defiance had leapt off her tongue. "No!" The thought of parading a range of outfits for Tareq's approval, having his eyes measuring their effectiveness, how well each garment fitted her figure...her stomach had cramped. She couldn't bear it.

Tareq had frowned at her vehemence. "I thought you would enjoy it." His frown had deepened. "There is also the matter of feeling at ease when we start mixing with others, Sarah." A quiet, gentle reasoning. "Inevitably, you will suffer considerable scrutiny as my companion. Critical scrutiny.''

Resentment at her enforced position had spilled out. ''And you'd prefer me not to look the little brown mouse at your side.''

His eyes had sparked with amusement. ''You're more a lioness than a mouse. Protecting your cubs.''

His reminder of the children made this even more a cat and mouse game to Sarah. Except Tareq wasn't a mere cat. He was a dangerous, dark, and very sleek panther, prowling around her, waiting to pounce, keeping her in almost intolerable suspense.

''It is irrelevant to me how you are dressed, Sarah,'' he'd declared. ''My main concern was to protect you from the bitchiness of other women. However, if you feel armoured enough against their barbs...''

She wasn't. She knew she'd hate being looked down upon, hate looking like a fish out of water. ''I do need some new clothes,'' she'd admitted grudgingly, then in a proud show of independence, had added, ''It's just that I want to go shopping by myself, choose them myself, and pay for them myself.''

To her intense relief he had let her do precisely that...after the embarrassment of having to accept the thirty thousand dollars he put in her credit account, a three months' advance on the salary he'd arbitrarily decided upon.

''But I don't do anything!'' she'd protested.

''That's for me to judge,'' he'd answered.

Recognising the futility of arguing, Sarah, nonetheless, had no intention of frittering away anything like that amount on clothes. Sam Bates had driven her to Naples, a shoppers' paradise with its many fashion boutiques, and she'd managed to find quite a few bargains amongst end of season stock that had been marked down.

Temporarily freed from the turmoil Tareq stirred, Sarah had enjoyed acquiring a range of clothes she felt really good in, assuring herself she didn't have to be competitive. As long as she was confident in her appearance, she'd be fine. Though she did wonder if Tareq was as uncaring about it as he said.

"Pleased with what you've bought?" he'd asked on her return to the house, eyeing the shopping bags with interest.

"Do you want to be shown?" she'd challenged.

He'd laughed, shaking his head. "I'll see soon enough."

But there'd been something—a cynical glint in his eyes?—that had made Sarah suddenly feel there'd been a purpose in letting her go shopping alone, a test in giving her so much spending power. The sense of being weighed on everything she did had her swinging from fierce belligerence—why should she care what he thought of her?—to sick panic, because she did care.

It was crazy to crave his good opinion, crazy to crave what could only be a self-destructive liaison with him. There might be physical satisfaction—even intense pleasure—in experiencing his sexual expertise, but there'd be humiliation, too, knowing she was letting down the ideals she'd clung to for so long. All the same, she hadn't known how strong carnal desire could be...its raging demands, its dreadful distraction, its power to pervert any normal thinking.

Sarah closed her eyes to the brilliant light of this new day, wishing she could shut Tareq out as easily. Maybe it would be easier with the company of other people around them, drawing his attention away from her. Looking at the horses he wanted to see had to be a diversion, too. The trip to Silver Springs might be less of an ordeal than she'd initially thought.

After all, she didn't know the people she'd be meeting. What they thought about her didn't really matter. Here today, gone tomorrow. Tareq was the unavoidable constant. Somehow she had to learn to live with the way he affected her.

A knock on the door. "Sarah?" *His* voice calling out.

Her eyes flew open. Her heart catapulted around her chest. She had to work some moisture into her mouth before answering. "Yes?" It came out high-pitched and quivery. He hadn't entered her suite all the time they were here. Was that about to change?

"There's a letter from Jessie. Do you want to come and read it?"

So much for her fevered imagination! On a wave of sheer delight, Sarah leapt out of bed, thrust her arms into her light silk wraparound to cover up her satin slip nightie, and raced to the door. She'd bought and sent postcards to Jessie and the twins but they couldn't have received them yet. It was a lovely surprise to get a letter so soon.

Her face was lit with happy anticipation as she opened the door, her smile spontaneous as she held out her hand for the expected envelope. Tareq grinned at her, his eyes taking in her dishabille and obviously savouring the lack of restraint apparent in her appearance. In sharp contrast, he was immaculately groomed and freshly clothed in body-hugging blue jeans and a white and navy Lacoste sports shirt.

Fighting a prickling sense of vulnerability, Sarah stared pointedly at his empty hands. "You said..."

"Tousled hair becomes you."

Was he checking how she looked first thing in the morning? Her teeth clenched. It was a non-effective action in stopping the rush of heat to her face. "Tareq..." she bit out.

"The letter came in on E-mail. You'll have to read it off the monitor screen in my study."

"E-mail?"

"Much quicker than the postal service."

Incredulity billowed over her confusion. "Jessie's using E-mail?"

"It's not difficult once you've learnt how. Follow me and I'll show you."

He set off, taking it for granted she would do as he dictated. Sarah hesitated, torn between having her curiosity immediately satisfied and wanting to bolt back into her bedroom and get properly dressed so she wouldn't feel at such a disadvantage. The drawcard of modern technology won over fears that seemed silly with Tareq's back already turned to her. Tying her belt firmly to prevent her gown flying apart, she trailed after him to the study which was furnished with every form of communication.

Tareq waved her to the swivel chair at his desk. The monitor screen above a computer keyboard glowed invitingly. Sarah could hardly believe her eyes as she sat down and began reading the printed script.

Dear Sarah,
I bet this surprises you. I'm writing this on my very own computer. It came the day after you left and a

tutor has been showing me how to use it. I can do drawings on it, too, and colour them any way I want. If I don't like one colour, I can use my mouse to change it to another colour. Isn't that marvellous? And so quick. Tareq said it would be a lot of fun and it is. It's the best present. Please thank him for me...

Her mind spun in shock. Her gaze jerked up to the man standing beside her. "You bought Jessie a computer? And lessons?"

He nodded. "Children take to computers very quickly. Here she is, up and running already," he said, clearly pleased with her progress.

"But why?" The extravagance of the gesture stunned her, even as she recalled the conspiratorial smiles he and Jessie had swapped, and his insistence that he kept the promises he made.

"I took you away," he answered with devastating simplicity. "This puts Jessie in easy touch and has the added benefit of keeping her well occupied. It's a great educational tool for a handicapped child."

Dear God! She had thought him ruthlessly manipulative while all the time he'd been thinking and planning how to help a crippled little girl over the absence of her big sister and give her something good to go on with.

"I'll show you how to reply once you've finished reading," he offered matter-of-factly.

She couldn't read. Her eyes were blurred with tears. She shook her head helplessly.

"Sarah?" He gently tilted her face up, his eyes questioning her distress.

"It's so kind...so generous," she choked out.

His mouth twisted into a self-deprecating grimace. "A

bit of thought, an order given, and the cost meaningless to me. Nothing compared to the two years you gave.''

"I love her." Reason enough to give anything.

"I know. After what happened to you as a child, it amazes me you didn't lose the capacity to love." He tenderly brushed his knuckles across her cheek. "I'm glad you didn't."

Her heart contracted at the sense of enticing possibilities hovering. "Did you lose your capacity to love?" she whispered, the softness of the moment prompting the impulsive question, the wish to reach into the inner man and know what he was truly made of.

Then suddenly the moment wasn't soft anymore. His hand dropped from her face, erasing the warmth. A hardness glazed his eyes. She could almost hear the armour he wore being locked into place. No cracks.

"Let's say it was whittled away very effectively," he answered sardonically. "To the point where I prefer horses to people. Horses are always beautiful. You can establish an empathy with them. And on the whole, they run true to form."

The cynical comment drove her to protest. "But you cared about Jessie."

"I always try to balance what I give and what I take, Sarah. I pride myself on playing fair."

"By whose rules?" she flared, afraid that what he might take from her could never be given back.

He laughed. "My own, of course. In the end, we have to live with ourselves so it's best to stay true to what we personally believe is right."

It was a sobering reminder of what she knew in her heart. Somehow she had to steel herself against the temptations inherent in being with Tareq al-Khaima.

There was no love on offer, only bargaining chips. If she didn't stay true to herself…yet what was true? Since she'd been with Tareq, a Sarah she hadn't known before was emerging, a stranger with needs that swamped common sense.

While Tareq—damn him!—was always in control.

"You don't need to stay. I know how to use E-mail," she said curtly, focusing her eyes on the screen again.

"Very well."

His withdrawal hurt, which was utterly stupid since she'd more or less asked for it. She tried to ignore the thud of his footsteps, concentrating fiercely on the words Jessie had written to her.

Please thank him for me…

She hadn't.

"Tareq…" She spun the chair around to face him.

"Yes?"

He paused in the study doorway, half turning to look back, so supremely composed, so arrogantly confident, so totally self-contained, so frustratingly untouchable, it stirred a wilful streak in Sarah that furiously dismissed the danger of courting trouble. He touched her whenever he felt like it. She wanted to know how he'd react if she touched him, if he'd still keep his armour intact.

Her feet sped across the room. Her hands lifted to splay over his chest. She went up on tiptoe. "A thank you from Jessie," she said, and kissed his cheek.

The next instant her hands were trapped by his, preventing their removal. Her palms were forcibly pressed to his body heat, transmitters for a sensory power that charged up her arms and exploded through her body, making every cell tingle with awareness of imminent and possibly cataclysmic change. His eyes blazed, scouring her soul of the petty vengefulness that had driven her, searing it with white-hot needs her mind could not even begin to encompass.

She stared back, helplessly caught in the thrall of his power, fearful of what she had triggered so heedlessly. She felt herself begin to tremble, shaken by the whirlwind of sensation beating through her. Her heart seemed to be thumping in her ears. Her breasts were swelling, tightening. A heavy, dragging feeling in her thighs was transforming into a melting heat.

Most shocking of all, he saw…he knew…and he said, "Don't tempt the devil unless you want to play with fire, Sarah."

Harsh, challenging words. No intent to seduce. No forcing anything. Demanding an unequivocal decision from her. And her memory spewed out the words… *I've never taken an unwilling woman to bed with me.*

Living by his rules…

Dear God! What were hers? How could they be so easily lost, overwhelmed? In sheer panic she clutched at safety. The alternative was too frightening.

She swallowed hard and forced out the one weak excuse for her behaviour she had. "I was only thanking you."

"Were you?"

Her skin burned.

The searing fire in his eyes slowly retreated to a mocking simmer. "So be it then. Consider me thanked."

He carried her hands down to her sides, released them, then walked away…a man of rigid principle.

Sarah was left feeling bereft…foolish…relieved. The truth was scorched indelibly on her brain. She could and had tapped into a furnace of feeling that would swallow her up if she opened the door to it. Touching was very different to loving, powerful but extremely perilous and not to be played with. Unless she wanted to be completely consumed by Tareq al-Khaima.

Surely that would be the ultimate madness.

Or would it be the ultimate experience?

CHAPTER EIGHT

TAREQ cursed himself for being a quixotic fool. He could have taken her then. He could have spun her into a sexual thrall so fast, resistance wouldn't have occurred to her. Instead, his body was screaming against the restraint he'd imposed on it.

For what? She wanted her curiosity satisfied. She wanted to know what he'd be like as a lover. She was so transparent...

And so was her innocence, he reminded himself savagely.

He headed out to the pool, stripped off and dived in, threshing through the cool water for several lengths, using up the explosive energy that had been denied its natural outlet. When he finally paused for breath, the needling tension had gone but he was still at war with himself.

He'd thought to give Sarah a good slice of life while he had the satisfaction and pleasure of knowing her in every sense. A fair exchange, he'd reasoned. She'd get to experience all she'd been missing out on and he'd enjoy giving her pleasure, showing her the world, being her teacher.

She was different to the women who usually peopled his life and he'd wanted to savour the difference. The bitter irony was the very difference that appealed to him, defeated the purpose he'd started out with.

It was cruelly obvious her loving heart would attach

more to sexual intimacy than the physical satisfaction he had in mind. If he took advantage of her vulnerability, how would they both feel about it afterwards? She'd already suffered a miserable pile of disillusionment in her life. He had a gut-recoil to adding another heap of it.

Yet he wanted her, wanted the full experience of her. He was so damned jaded, her freshness had a compelling appeal and with her giving nature, her artless honesty, whatever he had with her would be very special. He knew it and he wanted it more than anything he'd wanted for a long, long time.

So what the hell was he to do?

The quandary was killing him.

He had to find some way around it.

CHAPTER NINE

THE calm after the storm, Sarah thought ironically, sitting through breakfast with Tareq. His usual gentlemanly manner had been resumed without the slightest suggestion of strain. Sarah worked hard at holding a natural approach to today's activities, asking about the ranch they would be visiting, the horses that interested him, the people who owned them.

She fixed their names in her mind—Jack and Miriam Wellesly-Adams—suspecting the double-barrelled surname represented an amalgamation of two very wealthy families. She'd taken her cue from Tareq, dressing casually in jeans, a black pair which had a matching battle jacket she could wear if the afternoon turned cool. Her lime green polo-necked top went well with it. Since no critical comment was forthcoming from Tareq, Sarah concluded she was suitably attired, regardless of her hostess's fashion standards.

Although dinner this evening was somewhat trickier. She and Tareq were to be overnight guests. "Classy casual," he'd advised when she'd asked him what to pack for it. How classy and how casual were left undefined. Sarah hoped her new lemon pants-suit fitted the requisites.

Cluttering her mind with superficial details kept more fretful thoughts at bay. Sarah almost managed to pretend she felt no tension at all. Logic insisted that as long as she didn't touch Tareq, he would respect whatever distance she chose to hold. Pouncing was not on his agenda. He was playing a waiting game. Though if she let herself think about that, her nerves would start screaming again.

She was glad when it was time to go. She wanted to put the confrontation in his study behind her, a long way behind her, physically as well as mentally. Once they were on the road she could immerse herself in the role of travelling companion and hopefully find lots of distractions.

Tareq surprised her.

A gleaming red Cadillac convertible was sitting outside the house and Sam Bates was loading their overnight cases in the trunk. Sarah stopped and stared. They'd been riding around in a silvery grey BMW all week. This car had certainly not been in evidence. Anyone would have to be blind not to see such a flamboyant vehicle.

"Where did that come from?" The question spilled from her lips.

"I hired it for this trip," came the matter-of-fact reply.

Sarah shook her head. It made no sense to her. Tareq spared no expense on his comfort and convenience but she didn't have him tabbed as a show-off sort of playboy. The red Cadillac convertible shouted *Look at me! I'm king of the road!* She tore her gaze from the glittering, extrovert attraction of the car and searched Tareq's eyes for the purpose he had to have for it.

"Why?" she asked.

He grinned, totally disarming her and sending a flock of butterflies through her stomach. "For fun," he answered and held out the keys to her. "I thought you'd enjoy driving it."

"Me? But I can't, Tareq. I've never driven on the wrong side of the road."

He laughed. "Here it's the right side. And you won't find it a problem on the highway. You just drive along in a lane as you do at home."

She was torn between caution and temptation. "What if I make a mistake?"

"I'll be right beside you with advice and instructions."

Still she hesitated. "It will be much safer if you drive."

"Safe, Sarah?" His eyes sparkled a teasing challenge. "How very boring! Haven't you ever thought it might be fun to drive such a car with the sun on your face and the wind in your hair and the wheel in your hands?"

"Of course I have."

"So be brave. Take a risk. Do it. At least once in a lifetime."

She took the keys, took the risk and did it, embracing the exhilaration of zooming along the highway at the controls of a flashy convertible because it was fantasy-fun and such an extraordinary experience might never come her way again. For a while driving demanded all her concentration, but once she was accustomed to the car and the different use of the road, her mind started niggling at Tareq's motives again.

Was this another test?

Had she grabbed too quickly at the once-in-a-lifetime thrill which he had the means to provide? Seduction could come in many guises and unlimited wealth was a powerful lure. Scorning the offer of driving this extravagant toy might have been a more principled stand than accepting it. She didn't want him to think he could buy her.

On the other hand, he could be measuring her capacity to dare against the instinct for safety. He had made it seem wimpish to refuse. Perhaps he thought she'd wimped out this morning after kissing him and was seeing if she *would* take a risk on something she found sensually attractive.

On reflection, Sarah had to dismiss that idea. He would have arranged the hiring of this car beforehand, probably yesterday. All the same, there had to be some purpose behind getting it for her to drive. She certainly didn't believe it was the whim of a moment.

"What made you think of doing this for me, Tareq?" she asked, darting a glance at him.

She saw the beginning twitch of a smile but had to return her gaze to the road. Since it was impossible to watch for any changes of expression and be a responsible driver at the same time, she tried to listen for telling nuances in his tone of voice.

"It's one of life's innocent pleasures. I wanted you to have it."

"Why?" Was it completely innocent?

"Why not? I could do it. Therefore I did."

Like the computer for Jessie. But there'd been a reason for that. Sarah felt uncomfortable being the focus of his spending power. "You said this morning you try to balance what you give and take…"

"And you wonder if I'm giving you an innocent pleasure so I can take a wicked one." Dry amusement.

Her heart fluttered. "I'd rather know the price if there is one," she rushed out, wanting the truth, needing to know how he thought of her.

"No price, Sarah."

The flat, unequivocal statement left no ground for more questioning, yet she felt frustrated, wishing he would explain himself instead of letting her seethe in ignorance.

"Surely there can be prizes in being with me," he said quietly.

It sounded like an appeal. Sarah darted a glance at him. He caught it, jolting her with the intensity of feeling in his eyes; a disturbing cocktail of desire and a dark, personal damnation. She wrenched her gaze back to the road, struggling with the sense of having hit unexpected turbulence.

"You don't have to show me the prizes," she said, thinking they were undoubtedly balanced by penalties.

"Knowing them is part of our journey together. Only in knowing everything does a choice become clear."

"What choice do I have in our journey?" she tossed at him.

He laughed. "A multitude of them. All the time you are choosing how much to give me, how much to keep to yourself, how much you will take from me."

She flushed at the accuracy of the perception.

"It is interesting, is it not?" he teased.

"I'm glad you find it so," she grated, feeling she was being directed through hoops for his entertainment.

"Come now, Sarah. Wouldn't you say it puts an exquisite edge to our involvement with each other? We are not bored, either of us. Finding the right pieces of the jigsaw and fitting them together is exciting."

There had to be thousands and thousands of pieces of him. She imagined he would put her together in his mind much faster. "Well, I guess once you have the full picture, boredom will set in," she said dryly.

"Or will it be satisfaction?" he mused. "A picture of rare beauty can give endless satisfaction."

Beauty was in the eye of the beholder, Sarah thought, wondering just how demanding Tareq's eye was. "You may find the picture flawed."

"Flaws can have an individual charm. They can be more endearing than perfection."

Sarah sighed. She was no closer to knowing him and she resented his way of seeking knowledge of her. "I don't like the feeling of being tested."

"Were you not doing the same to me when you kissed me this morning?" he countered sardonically.

It was true in a way. Yet it had been more a driven impulse than a calculated plan. Testing him? She pondered the concept and decided it was alien to her. She wasn't cold-blooded enough to work out the equations and act on them as ruthlessly as Tareq did. Maybe that was something she had to learn if she was to survive a year with him intact.

"Be honest with me, Sarah," he urged, steel gloved in the softly persuasive tone of voice. "Was it not an experiment to test your touching power?"

Sarah instinctively recoiled from such cold, clinical terms. "Not in the way you mean," she protested painfully. "I was trying to reach out to you. To whatever it is you keep to yourself. I guess…in the light of how you reacted…that was very silly of me."

He made no comment. His silence dragged on for so long it grew heavy with a host of mulled-over variations of what he left unspoken. Sarah glanced at him but he wasn't looking at her. He appeared sunk in deep thought, his face an expressionless mask as he brooded behind it. For a few moments she exulted in the possibility his calculations had been upset. Then she realised there was nothing to be gained by it anyway. He was probably re-working his jigsaw to accommodate a rogue piece. Or maybe he was realising she didn't fit and would never fit into the picture he wanted.

She drove on in a miserable haze of despondency. Gone was the exhilaration of driving a convertible. The car ate up the miles just as every other kind of car did, moving from point A to point B.

"We're getting close to Ocala," she said matter-of-factly. "Is the exit to Silver Springs clearly sign-posted?",

"I'll point it out to you when it comes up," he assured her, alertness instantly galvanised.

The interstate highway had not exactly been a scenic route. However, once they'd turned off it and were heading towards Silver Springs, the beautiful countryside lifted Sarah's spirits. They passed one magnificent ranch after another; all of them with expensive railing fences enclosing pastures that looked like perfectly mown green lawns, picture postcard settings for the thoroughbred horses grazing in them. Even the grass verges on either side of the road looked mown, incredibly tidy if not. Wonderful trees, pleasingly placed, provided ready shade.

Such superbly maintained properties bespoke long-held wealth, used lavishly over generations. It was strange, comparing them to Michael Kearney's estate in Ireland and her father's farm in Australia...the amazing contrasts in style and form. What she was seeing here seemed distinctly American, with just as high a priority placed on appearance as on performance. Such attention to detail was truly marvellous.

The homesteads were just as breathtaking, mansions on a huge scale, fascinating in their stunning architecture. When Tareq pointed out their destination, Sarah couldn't help gasping. The Wellesly-Adams home could have graced one of the old Southern plantations; rows and rows of wonderful white columns, two storeys high, with verandas decorated by gloriously ornate, white lace ironwork.

The house alone seemed to offer a veritable Eden to explore and Sarah confidently anticipated ready distraction from Tareq and the stress of resolving their differences. There was no warning of a serpent within who would poison any peace of mind for her.

Their host and hostess could not have been more friendly and charming in greeting their arrival. Tareq and Sarah were graciously ushered into the vast foyer, basking in Miriam and Jack Wellesly-Adams' warm welcome. Then down a staircase designed for dramatic entrances, came a female cobra, all primed to strike.

"Tareq, darling…"

She was thirty-something with the patina of long-practised polish; long, gleaming blonde hair, a dazzling mouthful of white, white teeth, a sexy, sinuous body encased in orange lycra-satin shirt and slacks, belted brilliantly with graduated gold chains, gold bangles on her arms, gold hoops in her ears, gold slippers on her feet, but no gold ring complementing her orange fingernails.

"Dionne…this is a surprise!" Tareq responded. "Is Cal with you?"

"Hadn't you heard, darling? Cal and I separated

months ago. When Dad and Mimsy said you were coming today, I couldn't resist flying down from New York to say hello.''

She fell on him...kiss, touch, feel...busy hands and pouty lips...saying hello with neon lights flashing *I'm available and I'd just love to climb into your jeans.*

Sarah hated watching her in action. Tareq had warned her nothing stopped some women and she knew it. They just waltzed in and staked their claim. But the black violence ripping through Sarah's heart had nothing to do with reason. A primitive possessiveness was raging through her. She wanted to fly at the woman, tooth and claw, and fling her away from Tareq. She wanted to scream he belonged to her!

Above the frenzy of her feelings rose a sense of shock, of dawning horror. How could she care so much! The only tie she had to Tareq was that of being his hostage, and he had no tie to her at all. This obsession with him had to stop.

Yet she couldn't stem the tide of revulsion she felt at his failure to push Dionne away from him. He did absolutely nothing to stop the woman drooling over him. He didn't care. And that hurt. It hurt so much Sarah tried telling herself his laissez-faire attitude meant nothing.

She had witnessed such licentious greetings many times at her mother's parties. People on the high society circuit took such liberties for granted. It was part of the game of keeping irons in the fire and a keen eye on the main chance. Do I want this? Well, I'll just keep it warm in case I do.

Her stomach cramped. If Tareq thought like that...

"And who have we here?" Dionne trilled, snuggling herself around Tareq's arm as she judged it time to give some scant acknowledgment to his travelling companion. Her feline green eyes skated over Sarah, summing up the competition and dismissing it.

"Good heavens, darling! So young! Have you taken to escorting schoolgirls around the world?" Tinkling amusement. Flirty eyes. "No wonder you requested separate bedrooms."

"Dionne, you are embarrassing Sarah," her father chided, though he smiled indulgently at his *darling* daughter.

"Not at all," Sarah cut in, seething over the putdown. "Though perhaps Tareq…" she shot him a chilling, black-eyed blast "…might now take the time to introduce us."

The coolly delivered reprimand amused him. He unhitched himself from the clinging blonde and stepped slightly aside, using his now-freed arm to gesture from one to the other. "Sarah, this is Dionne Van Housen, Jack and Miriam's daughter, and until recently, the happy wife of a good friend of mine."

Dionne pouted playfully at him. "If Cal had made me happy, darling, I wouldn't have left him."

"That could be a comment on expectations being too high, Dionne," he said dryly. "May I introduce Sarah Hillyard, who was, indeed, a schoolgirl when I first met her, but that was eleven years ago. Happily, for me, time has moved on."

"Hillyard…Hillyard…should I know the name?" Dionne quizzed, prompting for Sarah's level of importance on the social register.

Tareq shrugged. "Unlikely. Michael Kearney was Sarah's stepfather during her teenage years. Her mother is now married to the Earl of Marchester."

Sarah burned with humiliation at being so labelled, as though her connection to the men in her mother's prize pile lifted her onto a more acceptable level. It revolted her even further that Tareq should feel the need to blow up her importance. Wasn't she good enough for him as she was?

"An earl! Doesn't that make your mother a countess?" Miriam Wellesly-Adams exclaimed, very favourably struck by this relationship with the English aristocracy.

She pounced on Sarah with the avid eagerness of milking a marvellous jackpot for all it was worth. Which neatly left Tareq to the eager come-ons of the snaky daughter all during the elaborate lunch, served in what was called the conservatory annexe.

Sarah hated every minute of it. Politeness demanded she answer her hostess's insistent and persistent questions on the English upper class, but she silently vowed never to suffer being put in such a position again. It was horribly false. Everything felt horribly false. How could a man feel the desire Tareq had shown her this morning, then toy with another woman? Where was the honesty in that?

Or maybe, since she hadn't made herself available, he simply and cynically took what was. After all, Sarah would keep. He had a whole year to play his game with her.

The luncheon dragged on. Tareq divided his time between talking horses with his host and responding to Dionne's demands for attention. The orange fingernails caressed his arm so often, Sarah began to wish they'd draw blood. It would serve Tareq right. She wanted him to feel as rawly wounded as she did.

It was almost four o'clock when they rose from the table, their host having suggested a visit to the stable yards was now timely. The offer to be transported by jeep was declined by Tareq who insisted a stroll would be more to his liking. A master of manipulation when he wanted to be, he persuaded Dionne into riding in the jeep with her parents and singled out Sarah as his walking companion.

Which suited Sarah just fine. It gave her the opportunity to lay down a few accommodations he could make for her in future. A hostage didn't have to be dragged everywhere. She was determined on loosening the tie with him. She had to for her own sanity.

As soon as the jeep was on its way, she dug her heels in and opened fire. "If you want to sleaze on with Dionne Van Housen, then count me out. I'll wait in my room until dinner."

Tareq turned to face her, one eyebrow raised in mocking amusement. "Sleaze on?"

"I find it disgusting. She's not even divorced from your *good friend*, Cal, yet, and you're letting her lech all over you."

"Since I've accepted the hospitality of her parents, what would you have me do, Sarah?"

"Oh, don't give me that excuse!" Her eyes blazed contempt for it. "You think I haven't been faced with stuff like that from my mother's high-flying crowd? It's easy enough to take a step back, offer your hand and maintain some personal dignity. The message gets across that liberties aren't welcome."

A smile twitched at his mouth. "Thank you for the lesson."

She huffed her exasperation. "You don't need lessons

in handling people. And you don't need me as a spectator for your little peccadilloes.''

He laughed. "I'm not the least bit interested in Dionne. But it is interesting that you have such a strong reaction against her liberties with me.''

The urge to slap his self-satisfied face was so strong, Sarah swung on her heel and marched off down the road to the stable yards, the other option of going to her room driven from her mind by the need to walk off the violence sizzling through her. Him and his damned jigsaw, fitting the pieces together! She was a human being, not bits of cardboard, and she would not be moved around for his entertainment!

He strolled along beside her, reforging the link she was desperately trying to repel. "From henceforth I shall keep other women at a distance,'' he declared. "Better now?''

"Better if you leave me out of these social occasions,'' she shot at him. "You don't value my company. Why bother with it?''

"If I didn't value it I wouldn't have sought your company for this walk. You have no reason to be jealous, Sarah.''

"It has nothing to do with jealousy,'' she lashed out in seething fury. "It's a matter of pride. I do not like being escorted by a man who lets himself be a target for loose women right in my face.''

"If you were indifferent to me, Sarah, it wouldn't matter. And with some women, other priorities would keep them silent and tolerant.''

"Well, stick to them if that's what you expect,'' she raged. "I don't want to be with you anyway. You're a snobby pig.''

"Ah! If this relates to my name-dropping, that was a ploy to cut dead any further patronising remarks."

"I don't care about patronising. People can be as patronising as they like and as far as I'm concerned it reflects badly on them, not me."

"It can still be upsetting."

"Oh, sure!" she mocked. "You're talking to a survivor of a toffee-nosed British boarding school where I was an Australian nobody. And let me tell you, Tareq al-Khaima, I don't need a name to prop me up as a person. I am *me*, no matter what I'm called, and if that's not good enough for you, then park me somewhere else when you want to mix with others."

"I'm delighted to be corrected on that point," he said quietly. "Such strength of character is so rare I wouldn't dream of parking you anywhere except beside me."

She shot him a baleful look. "Don't you ever, ever, attach me to Michael Kearney or the Earl of Marchester again. They don't turn me into something better. They diminish me."

"You're right. I'm sorry I did that to you, Sarah."

His agreement and apology stole the momentum of her fury. However, it didn't stop the sick churning of being with him and not being able to reach the heart of the man. Why did she care so much? How had he got to her so deeply? He shouldn't be able to do this to her when his caring was so insultingly shallow it didn't even begin to comprehend where she was coming from.

The all too transient pleasure of driving a convertible...

Protecting her from being patronised...

Luxuries on tap...

What good were they when her most innermost needs

craved what he was incapable of giving? He could keep his damned prizes for being with him in future! She wouldn't take any of them.

"I don't like you, Tareq," she stated bluntly, hugging in her hurt and wishing the intensity of feeling he stirred would go away.

"Perhaps, when you finish re-educating me, you'll like me better," he answered, a touch of whimsy in his voice.

It vexed her that he could take it so lightly while she was a torn up emotional mess. "Try being consistent," she muttered, shooting him a resentful glare. "Try being honest!"

He smiled at her...flooding her mind and heart and soul with the sweet, seductive warmth of approval and admiration, dazzling her with the beauty of it, the strength of it...tying her even more inexorably to him because he gave it.

CHAPTER TEN

TAREQ roamed around the sitting room of their hotel suite, pondering the situation as he waited for Sarah to finish dressing and emerge from her bedroom. This diplomatic visit to Washington had been scheduled long before he'd gone to Australia. Cancelling was out of the question. Sarah had to understand that Washington was an entirely different playground to Florida. Here, a united front had to be presented, regardless of what she felt towards him.

This dinner tonight marked the start of their public appearances and comment would flow from them. Sarah had to be brought into line with what needed to be projected... therein presenting Tareq with a tricky challenge since she had a mind of her own which was still set against him. Nevertheless, word of their togetherness would be relayed to his uncle and mixed messages would not put an effective block on the canny old man's political manoeuvrings.

It would have been so much simpler if they'd become lovers by now. Then staying at the embassy, which was his usual practice, would have established the relationship in the eyes of the staff, thereby making it very quickly known. As it was, taking up residence in the Oval Suite at the Willard-Continental was almost as good. It implied a desire for privacy in which to enjoy a new intimacy. Though he was fast coming to the conclusion there might never be physical intimacy with Sarah.

He'd really muddied his slate over that stupid business at Silver Springs. Letting Dionne Van Housen play with a flirtation had served as a distraction from his frustration, but it had cost him dearly, turning him into a lesser man in Sarah's eyes. An unlikeable man. And while he admired her high standards of integrity, they drew a line he found he couldn't cross. Not with an easy conscience.

Tareq shook his head self-mockingly. It was crazy, trying to live up to what she wanted him to be, yet he was doing it as best he could. The funny part was, it gave him a real buzz to win a smile from her, to feel warmth seeping past her guard. He liked being with her even if it was only company and conversation. He liked the purity of her thinking, the directness of her honesty. In that way, she was still the child he'd remembered.

Which put him into even more conflict.

The urge to look after her quarrelled with the constant desire to reach out and take her, make her his for as long as it worked for them. Yet as much as he told himself he'd be good for her, he couldn't quite dismiss the possibility he might end up hurting her. Badly. And hurting Sarah would be like hurting a child.

Don't make promises you don't intend to keep.

If she equated sex with a promise of love... a promise of commitment...

He couldn't lie to her.

Which left what... being honourable?

Tareq was grimacing at this unpalatable line of logic when Sarah made her entrance to the sitting room. Her appearance brought his pacing to an abrupt halt. It blotted out everything else on his mind. It shot a bolt of fire to his loins. It flipped his heart.

She looked utterly, stunningly beautiful, a picture of style and elegance, and so gut-wrenchingly sexy Tareq didn't trust himself to move. One step towards her and he'd be hauling her off to bed like a caveman.

"Will I do?" she asked, slowly pirouetting to give him the full effect of her outfit.

A long tunic made of some soft, clinging fabric moulded every line and curve of her figure like a second skin. The high round neckline and long sleeves accentuated the effect of a total body covering stretched around her flesh to faithfully outline her femininity. It was overwhelmingly sensual yet undeniably modest. Youthful.

The green floral pattern on a background of pure white had the fresh appeal of spring, and this was highlighted by a single white silk flower, perched on one shoulder, close to the curve of her throat. No jewellery to diminish the effect.

The tunic was slit on both sides to mid-thigh, and she wore long white satin trousers underneath it, giving an Eastern flavour to the outfit, making it even more alluring.

"Well?" she prompted, her eyes uncertain, seeking approval.

Her vulnerability pierced his heart. His plans—everything he'd thought in coming to some solution that would suit him—suddenly seemed terribly wrong. There was no clear course except... to protect her. Even from himself.

He took a deep breath, banking down the fire within. She was waiting for an answer. He should let her go...

out of his too complicated life... yet deep inside him screamed a need to keep her with him.

"Perfect!" he declared—a perfect torment of seductive innocence.

"I know it's right for me," she said artlessly. "I loved it from the moment I tried it on when I went shopping in Naples. But is it right for tonight?"

She would stand out like a spring flower amongst hothouse roses, Tareq thought, and the imagery instantly inspired the only course for him to take... if he was to keep her in his life... a bit longer anyway... long enough to make sense of everything.

"Perfect!" he repeated, smiling reassurance as he walked towards her. "You look so very lovely, I consider it an honour to be escorting you tonight."

She flushed at the compliment, pleasure warming her eyes.

He lifted one of her hands to his lips and bestowed a soft kiss of homage. Gallantry was not dead. Tareq had just resurrected it.

CHAPTER ELEVEN

London
14th December

Dear Jessie,
It hasn't snowed here yet but the weather people
are forecasting a white Christmas in England. It's
bitterly cold outside, much colder than Washington
and New York. Lucky for us, Tareq's house in
Eaton Place has good central heating. I do miss the
sun, though. I guess I was spoiled by the two
weeks we had in Florida.

SARAH STARED at the words on the computer monitor
screen and was struck by the sheer inanity of bumbling
on about the weather. It was what people did to evade
touching on anything more sensitive. It filled in space
that couldn't be filled with anything else. Certainly not
the truth. Impossible to confide the truth to a ten-year-
old child.

The acute sense of loneliness that she'd hoped to allay
by writing to Jessie became more acute. She was hopelessly in love with Tareq al-Khaima and there was no
one she could talk to about how she felt, no one she
could turn to for advice. Certainly not her mother.

The day after arriving in London she'd telephoned
Marchington Hall to ask that the clothes she'd left there
in storage be sent to her. Amongst them were her good

cashmere cape and some classic woollens that never went out of fashion.

"What number did you say in Eaton Place?" her mother had queried.

Sarah had repeated it and the Countess of Marchington had gloatingly pounced. "I know that address. It's Tareq al-Khaima's residence. What are you doing there, Sarah?"

There was no point in denial. Her mother was like a ferret when it came to finding out what she wanted to know about noteworthy people. "I met up with Tareq in Australia and he invited me to travel with him. I'm his guest at the moment," Sarah had rattled out, trying to make it all sound blithely innocent.

"What a clever girl you are! Do try to hang on to him, darling. He's fabulously wealthy. And so gorgeous!"

The avid note in her voice had been enough to turn Sarah off saying anything more. Everything within her recoiled from having what she felt tarnished by her mother's values. She'd swiftly ended the call, though she suspected her mother would now plot a meeting to check out the possibilities. That had to be blocked at all costs. It would be hideously embarrassing and humiliating.

Sarah gritted her teeth against a rise of bitterness and forced her mind back to the letter.

Washington...the word leapt out at her from the screen. She'd sent Jessie postcards of the White House, Arlington Cemetery, the Ford Theater where President Lincoln had been shot, the Air and Space Museum which had housed so many marvels from the first plane flown by the Wright Brothers to the Apollo space capsule carrying models of the astronauts; all the places she had visited during the day when Tareq was busy with meetings. But the nights...

It had been both daunting and exciting accompanying Tareq to the dinners and parties where his VIP status was awesomely in evidence. He was courted by politicians, lobbyists, diplomats, not to mention their wives who were very solicitous of his pleasure. No one mentioned horses or property developments. The oil markets and Middle East politics were the hot topics and Tareq handled them with an authoritative ease that demonstrated another dimension of the man.

He handled everything masterfully, from fending off fawning women to rescuing Sarah from sticky questions and ensuring she was not exposed to problems or unpleasantness by the simple but effective measure of not allowing anyone to take her from his side. Even prearranged places at tables were rearranged to accommodate his insistence on their not being separated.

It was stamped on every mind that Sarah Hillyard was to be respected as Sheikh Tareq al-Khaima's companion and under his protection and woe betide anyone who put a foot wrong with her or slighted her in any way. His manner to her was courteous, gentlemanly, above reproach in word and deed. In short, he treated her like a princess and subtly forced others to do the same.

It made her feel cosseted, valued, cared for as though she was precious to him. This was heightened by his air of possessiveness. Only he took her arm. Only he rested a light hand on her waist. Only he danced with her. It was heady stuff for Sarah who found it more and more difficult to keep her feet on the ground.

At first she had thought Tareq was treating her as he believed she wanted to be treated, a cynical display of his *re-education*. But there was nothing even slightly sardonic in his behaviour towards her. Then she had reasoned Washington was a hotbed of political gossip and Tareq's public performance was probably being reported to the embassy which served his country and thus back to his uncle. Perhaps she was being convincingly set up as the woman in his life so she would come as no surprise at his half-brother's wedding.

All she absolutely knew was Tareq eased off the act in private, remaining polite and considerate but holding a distance she could not cross. Some nights he parted very abruptly from her. Other nights he questioned her closely—Had she enjoyed herself? Was she interested or bored? Would she prefer not to be involved with such company?—and she had the chilling sense of more pieces being fitted into his jigsaw of her. What struck her more painfully than anything else was that once they were alone together, there was no physical touching, absolutely none.

Exhilaration...frustration. Sarah swung from one to the other like a yo-yo. She needed the daytime away from Tareq to regain some equilibrium. Yet still he shadowed her every hour. If she wasn't thinking of the evening before or the evening to come, she was thinking of what to share with him of her sight-seeing activities, how to be companionable while covering up the ever-constant desire of wanting more from him.

The same pattern had been repeated in New York, although there the meetings and dinners had been with bankers and the talk had revolved around the money markets. More new clothes had become a necessity. The between seasons outfits she had purchased in Naples simply didn't suit the New York winter and she was very conscious of not letting Tareq down in company.

They had flown to England a week ago, taking up residence in this house, and in some ways it had proved the most difficult time for her. There was nothing new about the city of London to distract her, no social engagements taking up the evenings, nothing to busy her in the house since a married couple looked after everything. And highlighting her failure to reach into Tareq's heart, was Peter Larsen, the person who knew him better than anyone.

The trusted trouble-shooter was already in London when she and Tareq had arrived. Whether he had flown directly to England from Australia, Sarah didn't know and didn't ask. Peter Larsen practised British reserve and discretion to the nth degree. He never spoke of business in front of her, despite spending most of each day at Eaton Place, either in this office which she presently occupied, or in the library where he was currently closeted with Tareq, discussing some business strategy.

He shared lunch with them, was unfailingly polite to her, and kept his own private life extremely private. The only personal thing Sarah knew about him was he owned an apartment overlooking the Thames.

She couldn't say she disliked him. He gave her no reason to. But she deeply envied the easy rapport between him and Tareq. Sometimes they talked in a kind of shorthand, their understanding so closely attuned, a look or a gesture conveyed more of a message than words.

Since the incident with Dionne Van Housen, Tareq had given Sarah no cause to be jealous of other women, but she *was* jealous of what he shared with Peter

Larsen. Their communication didn't miss a beat and the bond of trust was so strong neither ever paused to question it. Somehow it turned her into an outsider, despite being in the same room as them.

Sarah heaved a despondent sigh and dragged her attention back to the letter she had started. She had no heart for it but she tried to find something more to say.

I'm glad the parcel from New York arrived safely and the twins had such fun at school with the Statue of Liberty hats.

The symbol of freedom. Would she ever feel free of Tareq, even when the year was over? She hoped her father was making the best of a fresh start because she was surely paying for it.

The office door opened, startling Sarah out of her reverie. Peter Larsen stepped into the room, carrying a file of papers. He paused, frowning slightly as he saw her occupying the chair in front of the computer. Sarah leapt up, gesturing an apology as she sought to excuse herself.

"I was writing to Jessie. I hope you don't mind my being here while you were with Tareq."

He shrugged. "As I understand it, you have the freedom of the house, Miss Hillyard. Do continue your letter if you so desire."

"I don't want to be in your way."

"I have only to return this file to the cabinet and then I'll be leaving." He surprised her by asking, "How is Jessie?"

"Fine! Looking forward to Christmas."

He smiled. Actually smiled. "Such a bright little girl.

She took to the computer like a duck to water. I liked her very much. Say hello to her from me.''

Sarah was quite stunned by this unexpected crack in Peter Larsen's customary reserve. ''Yes, I will,'' she answered, dazedly watching him cross the room to the filing cabinet before it occurred to her to remark, ''I didn't know you'd met her.''

He answered matter-of-factly as he took a set of keys from his trouser pocket, unlocked the cabinet and pulled out a drawer. ''I made a point of it after my last meeting with your father. Mainly to check her progress, see that the tutor was doing his job well and Jessie was happy with what she was learning.'' He glanced at Sarah, smiling again. ''She insisted on demonstrating her new skills to me so I could tell Tareq how good she was.''

A child like Jessie could bring warmth out of a stone, Sarah thought. Hoping this was an opportunity to milk Peter Larsen of more information on her family, she asked, ''How long ago was this?''

''Just before I flew out,'' he replied, inserting the file in the drawer. ''First of December.''

Sarah totted up the time he'd spent in Australia after she and Tareq had left. Four weeks. Which seemed an excessive amount.

''Was my father holding up okay?'' she asked anxiously. ''I mean…were you satisfied he was doing the right thing by the horses and everything?''

''I was satisfied your father had every good intention, Miss Hillyard.'' He gave her a sympathetic look. ''You must know that only time will bring results.''

''Yes. of course. It was just… I was worried about Firefly…and his poor performance in the Melbourne

Cup." She cast around for a way to ask if her father had displayed any particular attitude towards the prize horse.

"It's been taken care of, Miss Hillyard. I saw to it personally. There'll be no more trouble coming from that quarter," Peter Larsen quietly assured her, then proceeded to relock the cabinet.

Sarah's concerns were far from answered. Had Peter Larson taken Firefly to another trainer? But that would defeat the test of Firefly's performance at the end of the year.

"How has it been taken care of?" she cried. "I don't see how..."

"Miss Hillyard, it's quite irrelevant how." There was a ruthless cast to the face Peter Larsen turned to her. "Rest assured the bookmaker who was squeezing your father has been convinced that any further attempt at dirty dealing with Tareq's horses would be very bad business. Extremely bad business."

Sarah's mind was reeling. All her assumptions were knocked in a mushy heap and what was emerging was too repulsive to accept. Dread clutched her heart, yet she had to ask, had to look at the can of slimy worms Peter Larsen had opened up. She could barely get her voice to work. The words came out faintly, strained through a welter of emotional resistance to hearing an even more damning statement.

"Are you saying my father threw races for a bookmaker?"

The satisfaction in the light silvery eyes blanked into shock. "Tareq didn't tell you?"

Sarah felt the blood draining from her face. "It wasn't just loss of heart and...and stress..."

"But you must know," he argued, more to himself

than to her. "Surely Tareq asked me to leave so he could tell you in private how far your father had abused his trust…"

He was recalling the morning at the Como Hotel, the fateful morning when the bargain had been struck. It rushed back on Sarah, too. "Why did he keep it from me? If my father was crooked…taking bribes…"

Peter Larsen passed a hand across his face, muttered something vicious to himself, then recomposed his expression to impervious reserve. "I do beg your pardon, Miss Hillyard. It seemed reasonable to set your mind at rest."

"Please… I want to know…"

"You must excuse me. I have been unforgivably indiscreet."

It was true then. Had to be. It was written all over Peter Larsen as he strode from the room, tight-faced, stiff-backed, patently appalled at what he had let slip to her. He'd almost certainly go straight to Tareq and relay what he'd done. And then what?

Sarah felt sick. Tareq's words came spinning back to her…*a matter of trust*. Trust abused beyond trusting again. And Tareq knew it. Had known all along while she'd pleaded a case for lenience, for understanding, for mercy on a man who, unbeknownst to her, had criminally cheated him.

He'd sent Peter Larsen out of the hotel room right at the moment when he should have revealed the truth. If he had gone ahead and done it, as Peter had assumed, the result would have been… Sarah concentrated hard on thinking back, remembering her state of mind. The truth would have swept the mat out from under her feet, would have smashed any grounds for giving her father a second chance. She would have died of shame and given up, faced with her father's crooked dealings with a bookmaker.

But Tareq hadn't wanted that result. He had posed the bargain, pressing her to accept, using his knowledge of her, using everything at his command to get her to accept.

For what purpose?

In the light of all that had followed in these past six weeks with him, Sarah still didn't know. Tareq had her so confused, it was driving her crazy wondering what he wanted of her. She was sick to death of his testing and teasing and tantalising behaviour. She wanted answers. And she was going to get them.

Now!

CHAPTER TWELVE

SARAH didn't bother knocking. Nothing was going to stop her from having a showdown with Tareq. She opened the library door and marched in, breathing fiery determination.

Peter Larsen swung around, opening a clear view of his employer friend, seated at the splendid mahogany desk he favoured. Sarah ignored the trusted trouble-shooter, her gaze fastening directly on the sharp blue windows to Tareq al-Khaima's unfathomable soul.

"I want to talk to you. Alone. And without delay," she stated, unshakably intent on getting her own way. Tareq was not going to dominate this encounter!

He rose from his chair, languidly unfolding to his full height, insufferably confident of controlling everything. "Thank you, Peter," he said, not the slightest trace of any acrimony in his tone. "I'll see you tomorrow."

Of course there was no cause for Tareq to be upset by the indiscretion, Sarah savagely reasoned as Peter Larsen took swift leave of them. The bargain had been struck and there was no going back. Tareq was sitting pretty on whatever he was sitting on. Except he wasn't sitting anymore. He was strolling around the desk. By the time the door behind Sarah was closed, he was propped casually against the front edge of the desktop, perfectly at ease.

The urge to smash his smooth facade raged through Sarah. How many deceptions was he juggling in the super-clever mind behind that handsome face? The feeling of being a pawn in a game she was not allowed to see put a violent edge on her churning emotions.

"I wouldn't have asked you to cover up criminal activity," she hurled at him. "If I'd known my father was intentionally cheating you, I would not have come to you at all."

"But you still would have wanted what you did achieve, Sarah," came the perfectly chosen pertinent reply. "Your father given a chance to redeem himself, and the security of the children assured as far as it can be."

In other words, everything else should be considered irrelevant. Sarah dug in her heels. "And just how far have you gone to achieve that, Tareq? How far do you go to get what you want?" she demanded heatedly.

He replied with calm logic, completely unruffled. "I find that people usually listen to reason when the profit and loss are laid out to them. Irrefutable facts do have impact."

"You withheld facts from me," Sarah pointed out, her eyes flashing resentment at his cavalier way of doing what suited him with her.

"I didn't want to hurt you," he said with heart-twisting simplicity. "You were innocent, Sarah."

But she *was* hurt, hurting non-stop from his keeping things from her and his arbitrary withdrawals that drove her into a deep trough of frustration. This confrontation wasn't really about her father. It was about attitude and honesty and the direction of this journey they were supposed to be taking together.

"I'm not a child, Tareq," she protested. "I'd rather be faced with the truth than be protected from it."

The moment the words were out, Sarah was struck by

the realisation that Tareq had been treating her like a child all along, a grown-up one to some extent, but still to be indulged and protected as though she were a complete innocent.

"What good would it have done?" he asked.

"I don't need you to make judgments for me. Nor decisions," she retorted, smarting over how many things had been arranged for her—without discussion—by her self-appointed keeper. "It's so intolerably patronising!"

"Sarah…" he chided.

"Don't use that tone of voice to me," she exploded, hating the sense of being relegated to some lesser level of understanding. "What right do you think you have to take over my life as though you know best?"

That stopped him from giving his soothing little smile. His eyes glowered, some dark emotion climbing over sweet reason. "I have tried to do my best by you, Sarah," he growled. "If you don't appreciate it…"

"Why don't you try appreciating I can think for myself?" she retaliated, cutting off his self-serving argument, finding it so intensely provocative, she stormed off around the room, savagely muttering, "Doing his best for me. Doing his best. Doing his best."

It didn't matter that it was probably true. It was what a parent said to a child. Her frustration with their relationship boiled over. She glared at him—this man who held himself back from her while subtly laying siege to her heart—and the need to strip him of his formidable control clawed through her.

"You obviously see me as a little girl to be pampered and given treats," she mocked, her hands flying around in scornful gestures. "Never mind that I'm twenty-three years old and a hardened survivor. I'm probably still twelve in your mind.''

That straightened him up from the desk and whipped some tension through him. A primitive satisfaction zinged through Sarah. She wished she could rip his clothes off, get right down to the naked truth of how he felt about her. The remembered image of his almost-bare physique played through her mind, stirring a wanton excitement, a wild desire to goad him into action, any action that involved touching.

''You are being ridiculous!'' he said tersely.

''Am I? You don't credit me with a woman's needs, a woman's feelings, a woman's desires. *'Don't play with fire, Sarah,'''* she mimicked. ''Just stand by and watch the sophisticated grown-ups like Dionne Van Housen play with it because they understand it and you don't.''

His face darkened with an angry rush of blood and Sarah exulted in having reached and plucked a sensitive chord. It flashed through her mind she wasn't being completely fair, but she was on a wild, non-stop rollercoaster, her nerves screaming with frustration, heart pumping with rushes of adrenalin, thoughts careering down the track he had chosen for her, the track that kept her at arm's length from him.

''Then there was Washington,'' she plunged on, gesticulating with mocking emphasis as she interpreted his actions. ''Trotting me out like a young debutante, protecting me from other men, saving me from any little awkwardness, watching over me like a father.''

His mouth compressed.

To Sarah, it denoted she'd hit the nail on the head and she heedlessly hammered it further, furious he'd denied her the maturity she knew she could lay claim to.

"You even dictated when I should go to bed, saying goodnight when it suited you. Same in New York. And here, of course, you've had the relief of adult company with Peter Larsen. It's a wonder you haven't given me dolls to play with."

"Are you quite finished with this absurd tantrum?" Tareq demanded, his eyes glittering with barely suppressed anger.

Tantrum...

The word stopped Sarah in her tracks. She shuddered in revulsion. A child threw tantrums. She had delivered a tirade of truth. Close enough to truth anyway. For Tareq to interpret it as a tantrum...

She drew in a deep breath. Her eyes stabbed him with daggers of pain as she made the only decision she could make. Then with all the passion of her womanhood, she replied, "I'm finished with you, Tareq. Since you treat me as though I haven't reached the age of consent, our bargain is null and void and I am out of here!"

Having flung down the gauntlet she turned her back on him and marched to the door.

"Wait!" he thundered.

"What for?" she flung back at him, throwing out dismissive hands. "I don't need another father. I've already had three. Between them they've done a fine job of ripping away any innocent illusions I might have had about life, so you don't have to worry about me being hurt. Henceforth I am a cynical woman of the world who doesn't believe in anybody."

She twisted the knob and pulled the door open. Before she could step out of the library an arm reached past her and slammed the door shut. Startled, she did nothing to stop the strong brown hand from dropping to the knob and activating the locking device. Her mind grasped the consequence though, and in the next instant she was whirling around to contest it, rebellion rampaging through her heart.

"I will not be your prisoner!" she yelled, her hands slamming against Tareq's broad chest in violent rejection of any more domination from him.

"Shut up!" he retorted fiercely.

The shock of it snapped her eyes up to his.

"You want raw truth?" he demanded, his voice harsh, his nostrils flaring, the windows to his soul revealing chaotic conflict. "I'm a man with a man's needs. And those needs don't come wrapped in finer feelings. How ready are you to accept that, Sarah?"

Dark turbulence enveloped her, sucking the strength from her mutiny, swirling around her thwarted desires, fanning them into a ferment of need, tearing at the feelings that had made being with him a torment, transforming them into something more intense, overwhelming, flooding her with a warm, liquid weakness, and she knew she would accept anything of him. Anything...

Somehow he saw what was happening to her, recognised it, and his arms swept her strongly against him, and the tremulousness inside her gathered a hunger for his strength. She pressed closer, her hips against his, needing, wanting, her hands sliding up over his shoulders, around his neck, her breasts pushing into soft, no hard, harder contact with the pulsing wall of his chest, pursuing the need, the want as a whirlwind of beating, throbbing sensation travelled through her.

The storm in his eyes was rent by a blaze of blue lightning, electrifying the air, tingling her skin, her lips, jolting her heart. Her mouth fell open, gasping for breath. Her mind seized on the image of his face, his beautifully sculptured face, coming nearer, nearer to hers. Her fingers raced into his hair, clutching, grasping, pulling his head nearer still. Every atom of her energy was focused on drawing him to her, reaching into him.

Then his mouth covered hers, softly at first, gently, tenderly, holding back the fire she'd seen and sensed and invited, but the heat of his lips, the caress of his tongue, the excitement of touch and taste whirled her into a passionate searching for all he would give of himself. Her whole body seemed to soar with exultation as he abandoned softness, driven to a wild exploration that eclipsed hers with its ardent, urgent hunger to know, to feel, the wanting a sweet, fierce, nearly desperate need, crying out to be satisfied more fully, more deeply.

Kissing was not enough. Kissing was an anticipatory intimacy, a tantalising promise, a binding beginning to the journey towards the togetherness she craved.

He moved her back against the door, holding her there between his thighs, the burgeoning thickness, hardness of his arousal stroking across her stomach in a rhythmic swaying as his mouth continued to devour hers, the need of a man implicit, raw, demanding to be met. His hands moved quickly, skilfully, stripping her of blouse and bra, dragging off his shirt, freeing flesh to meet flesh, heated with feverish excitement.

Then he was kissing her breasts, his tongue circling the nipples, teasing them into needful erection, and Sarah threw back her head, arching to push for more acute sensation, the need of a woman surging through her, concentrating fiercely on the hot attachment of his lips, sucking, dragging an intense stream of pleasure through her body, her flesh pulsing to his pumping mouth, his hands stroking her thighs, rolling down her trousers, fingers smoothing her stomach, thrusting through moist curls to the core of heat, cupping it, taking possession of the wet softness.

Sarah closed her eyes and gave herself up to the sweet chaos of sensation, forgetting everything, all sense, all caution, all care, wanting only to feel. She had no idea how Tareq accomplished the rest of their undressing. Her entire physical existence was turned inwards to the hunger he fed with his skilful touching, the seductive, exquisitely pleasurable invasion of hand and mouth.

Only when he picked her up and carried her did she realise she was naked, both of them naked, and the sensuality of skin against skin was another wonderful intimacy. He lay her on the soft Persian carpet in front of his desk and she feasted her eyes on him as he knelt over her, such powerful maleness poised to mate with her, and her body was crying out for him, longing to feel him there in the place that was made for him.

She lifted her arms and he came into them, kissing her mouth, slowly, tenderly, as she felt him pressing against her, beginning to fill the opening to her charged, innermost self. Her whole body quivered in waiting. She moved, urging him on, thrusting for the fullness of him inside her. His hands slid beneath her, holding, moulding her buttocks and she felt him enter, slowly pushing further, growing, and she had the amazingly voluptuous sensation of opening before him, spilling the essence of herself around his passage, muscles pulsing, drawing him in.

She heard herself cry out sharply when he stopped. But it was only a pause to negotiate a barrier neither of them wanted. A pinprick of pain and it was past, trailing in the wake of deep, deep pleasure as he sank into ecstatic union with her, and she curled her legs around him to hold him in, savouring the sense of him being captured, possessed by her, a prisoner enveloped, held in a sea of intense bliss.

His mouth took hers in a long passionate entanglement, making the possession his, and she surrendered to it, letting him do as he willed because it didn't matter. Only the togetherness mattered. And he led her on a journey she had never taken before, a wild, plunging ride of ever-increasing excitement, rising to an exhilarating peak, falling only to rise again, on and on, a tumult of sensation, tumbling endlessly, spreading out into everwidening, powerful circles, faster, faster, drawing her into a vortex that spiralled towards a brilliance she couldn't quite reach.

Frantically she thrust at him, pulling him with her, needing his help, arching her body to drag him into it, a fierce compulsion driving her, driving him, and there was thunder in her ears, white-hot needles piercing her body, pain-pleasure screaming for release, and she needed it, needed it, him with her, riding the crest of…and there it was, an explosion of exquisite sweetness bursting through her like a supernova, and she was floating in an incredible free fall, swimming in waves of love, her heart thumping a paean of joy, her mind filling with the wonder of it, her body sinking into blissful quiescence.

She opened her eyes and Tareq was looking at her, drinking in the soft glow of her repletion, knowing he had put it there, a tender triumph in his eyes. "This I can give you," he said, his voice low, throaty, husking over feelings that were inexpressible.

Gently he stroked her cheek, traced the desire-swollen fullness of her lips, kissed them, kissed her eyelids shut again. Then with a long, hissing sigh, he gathered her to him, lifting her as he moved aside to lie on the carpet, using his body to cushion hers, holding her to the warm closeness of intimate contact.

He stroked her hair, her back, languorous caresses that kept her sensually aware of both herself and him. Sarah was lost to everything else. He was her world. She rose and fell to the rhythm of his breathing. The drum of his heart echoed her own. She wanted for nothing. He had given, was still giving, more than she had ever imagined he would.

"Is it enough?" he asked, his voice oddly strained.

It stirred her sluggish mind out of its comfortable haze of pleasure. He had fulfilled her needs, but she simply did not have the experience to know if he was completely satisfied. What if she had been hopelessly inadequate in returning his lovemaking? Should she have been more active towards him instead of being so utterly enthralled by her own feelings? Did he feel shortchanged?

"Do you want more?" she asked in reply, her heart fluttering at the thought she had failed him.

His hands splayed possessively over the pit of her back. He gave a funny little laugh. "More and more and more. I would take all you would let me have, Sarah. Until there is no more."

She smiled, comprehending that he was pleased with what they'd shared and he was looking beyond the moment, further down the path they had taken today.

"Yes," she agreed, anticipating the filling in of all

that had been missing in her knowledge of him. "I want that, too."

He sighed, his whole body relaxing underneath hers. "So be it then," he murmured. His arms enfolded her, wrapping her tightly to him as he turned them both onto their sides. His eyes locked onto hers, a glitter of purpose in their dark blue depths. "You stay with me of your own free will," he stated, commanding her assent.

"Yes," she answered, thinking he was dismissing the hostage arrangement and making it a purely personal decision to stay with him, not for her father, not for Jessie and the twins, for herself alone, because she wanted to. "Yes," she affirmed more emphatically.

The glitter flared into the all-consuming blaze of desire she had seen weeks ago when he had challenged her willingness to accept it. Now it was unleashed on her and she revelled in it, meeting his mouth, kissing him as avidly as he kissed her, sealing the new bargain between them.

She didn't realise that being lovers was all he had in mind, didn't realise the pact she'd just made had limits, didn't realise promises would not be given because too much stood in the way of their being kept.

She loved him and felt loved by him.

It was more than enough.

At this moment in time.

CHAPTER THIRTEEN

ALL morning Tareq had struggled to direct his mind onto the business decisions to be made before the festive season closed everything down. The Persian carpet in front of his desk was a constant distraction. The searing memories of yesterday…last night…continually kicked at the control he was valiantly attempting to assert over the desire that tempted him to toss his responsibilities aside and indulge himself in every possible pleasure with Sarah.

He read the invitation that had come in the mail with a certain amount of cynical amusement. It was addressed to him and was from the Earl and Countess of Marchester. Sarah's society-minded mother was undoubtedly intent on showing off her daughter's *conquest* at a formal dinner on Christmas Eve.

Irrelevant to him whether they attended or not, but it was Christmas, and mothers were mothers. He would be visiting his own, as expected, on Christmas Day. It was up to Sarah to decide what she wanted to do.

I don't need you to make judgments for me. Nor decisions.

He shook his head over his own misjudgments. Sarah was so young, yet very much a woman who knew her own mind and with courage enough to seize what she wanted and run with it. The passion of her, the wilfulness and wantonness, the intense response from her… Tareq marvelled at it.

The invitation from her mother provided a valid excuse to seek her out, to be where he most wanted to be...with her. "This bit of mail is for Sarah," he said to Peter Larsen who was diligently scanning other correspondence. "I'll take it to her."

Peter looked up, concern drawing his eyebrows together as Tareq rose from his chair. "Is she okay? I do regret having upset her yesterday."

"Not a problem. In fact, it worked out very well."

The satisfaction underlining the remark evoked a quizzical look from Peter.

Tareq ignored it. His private life was private. And compellingly attractive. He made a swift decision. "We finish this paperwork today, Peter. Prioritise what absolutely needs to be done. I'm taking time off until we have to prepare for the trip to the homeland. The second week in January should cover the reports my uncle will expect."

"Suits me," he agreed, keeping his curiosity contained.

Having released himself from work that could wait, Tareq had an even more buoyant spring in his step as he went in search of Sarah. He found her in the sitting room, curled up on the sofa closest to the hearth where a cosy fire was alight. She was reading a book and he noted a pile of books on the table next to the sofa.

So engrossed was she in the story, his entrance had gone unnoticed, and he paused before disturbing her, remembering her scathing comment about giving her dolls to play with. He was well aware Sarah was far too intelligent to be content with a frivolous life. Nursing a child with Jessie's disabilities had obviously been rewarding and the time would come when she would crave another challenging occupation.

Time…it was always going to be the enemy for them. The thought stirred an urgent greed for all he could take now, while it was new and good and untainted by the conflicts that would inevitably part them.

She was so lovely…every aspect of her.

As though sensing his presence, she glanced up, her dark chocolate eyes sparkling with delight when she saw him. "Why are you standing there?"

"Just remembering how you looked when I took up your breakfast tray this morning."

She blushed but newly bold mischief curved her luscious mouth. "Naked and tousled is not exactly appropriate for the sitting room."

"I had no problem with it in the library." He closed the double doors behind him, ensuring uninterrupted time together.

Her eyes widened, disbelief that he would repeat their lovemaking here warring with excitement as he crossed the room to where she sat, squirming slightly at his approach, revealing a desire as strong as his, a consciousness of aroused sexuality. He saw her breasts peak, hardened nubs pushing out the soft, clingy fabric of her shirt, and though he'd only intended talking to her, the urge to touch and revel in the freedom to touch zinged through him like a strong intoxicant.

"We have an invitation to Marchington Hall," he said, holding out the embossed card to her.

She fumbled her book onto the table and took the card to read it. He lifted her curled legs and sat beside her, laying her legs across his lap, stroking them, savouring the feminine grace of their long curves. The fine black tights encasing them made them even more sensually alluring. Her ankle-length skirt was buttoned down the side, a tantalising row of little openings offering further temptation.

"A formal dinner," Sarah groaned. "It's sure to be a five-star production and my mother will make you the showpiece, Tareq. She thinks…"

The pause in her speech drew his attention and the look of confusion in her eyes reminded him quite poignantly that she was not a hardened sophisticate, and while she might want and accept their relationship, it left her very vulnerable to other, more cynical views of what they shared.

"Do you mind her seeing that we're lovers?" he asked.

"No, of course not. I'm not ashamed of what I feel," she replied strongly, another flush colouring her cheeks. "It's just… I guess I'm not used to the idea yet. And I resent her thinking I set out to hook you and get what I can out of you. As it is, she'll take one look at us and think she was right."

The boot was on the other foot, Tareq thought with a twinge of guilty conscience. He had set out to hook Sarah and get what he could from her. Though it was different now, he quickly assured himself. He wanted to give, wanted her to have everything within his power to give.

"We don't have to go, Sarah. It's your choice. I'll have no compunction whatsoever in writing a refusal."

She heaved a sigh which drooped into a rueful grimace. "I haven't seen my mother for two years. We had a huge argument over my decision to help with Jessie.

I wish I could believe she really wanted to see me, and not because I'd have you in tow.''

"Maybe she does," he said, responding to the sadness he sensed in her. "Once there's a deep rift, and communication is difficult to re-establish, it's an easier situation to meet in the company of other people. Less chance of another blow-up.''

It prompted an ironic smile. "You mean nothing really gets said in a crowd.''

He shrugged. "There is still comfort in seeing a person you care about. At the very least, it's a check on their well-being. As you said, it's been two years.''

And he didn't like to think of her being completely cut off from her mother. Even tenuous links to her family were worth keeping. There was no joy in feeling alone in the world. He wished he could promise their togetherness would last and she would never again be alone, but the realities of his life made nonsense of any such assurance.

"Perhaps we should go," she said uneasily. "It is Christmas. My mother and I don't see eye to eye on much, Tareq, but I guess it would be mean not to at least show goodwill.''

"No harm in it," he agreed. "I'll send an acceptance then.''

Her eyes were anxious, embarrassed. "Will you mind if she gloats over our connection?''

He laughed. "I may very well do some gloating myself. No other woman can hold a candle to you, Sarah.''

It made her laugh. "I'm glad you think so but my mother won't.''

"Oh, yes, she will." The hard-core protective instinct she had evoked in him all along was instantly tapped.

No one was going to slight Sarah while he was at her side. The anticipation of many pleasures buzzed through him as plans formed in his mind.

"Tomorrow we fly to Paris. I'll take you shopping. I shall drape you in splendour from head to toe, and no one will shine more brightly."

She fluttered towards him in agitated protest. "I don't want you to buy me things, Tareq."

He scooped her down on the sofa and swiftly repositioned himself to lean over her, imprisoning her legs with his. "Why would you not want to celebrate being a woman with me?" he asked, gently brushing wayward curls from her forehead, kissing the tip of her nose, flirting wickedly with his eyes, drawing his hand slowly along the inner sides of her thighs, feeling the excited quiver of her flesh under his touch. "You are an incredibly beautiful woman and I want you to know it and feel it and enjoy it."

Her breath shuddered out and her breasts rose enticingly as she dragged in more air. "People will know it's your wealth dressing me, Tareq. It will look as though…as though…" Her voice trailed off uncertainly and he knew her body was tensely poised, waiting for his hand to move higher.

"As though I cherish you," he finished for her. "I want to give you the best, Sarah. The best of everything." He fanned his fingers over the soft nest at the apex of her womanhood and slid his thumb down the cleft, stroking with all the seductive skill at his command. "I want to dress you in satins and silks and velvet…which is how you feel to me…smooth and soft and sensual…"

Her stomach contracted. Her lips parted in a little

gasp. He swept his tongue around them then kissed her, plundering her mouth of its infinitely sweet giving, revelling in her uninhibited response, feeling it flow through him, arousing the power to take her on any journey he desired.

"I find you utterly intoxicating, Sarah," he murmured, brushing her lips with his words, their breaths mingling in heated intimacy. "I see you dressed in wine red, a dark fire glowing, like the fire burning in me...for you..."

"I only need you, Tareq," she pleaded.

It put a twist in his heart. He almost lost it then, his need for her a thunder that almost obliterated all rationality. But he couldn't let her need him to the exclusion of everything else. There had to be other avenues for her, roads she could take with confidence. There would be a cost to the relationship she had chosen with him and it had to be made up. He had to supply her with the means to go on without him, though he hated the thought of losing her.

"Would you deprive me of the pleasure of giving?" he pleaded in reply, trailing kisses to her ears, pausing to erotically sensitise each lobe. "I want to hang rubies here...red-blood rubies...because you're in my blood..." He dropped his head, sucking briefly on the pulse at the base of her throat. "...And a necklace of rubies...precious jewels to show you are precious to me."

Her back arced, her distended nipples pointing provocatively. Uncaring of the fabric covering them he tugged on each inviting peak with his teeth, heating them with his mouth, exulting in her little moans of excitement, the threshing of her body in seeking more intense pleasure.

"I'd have these beautiful breasts encased in soft swirls of French lace..." He bit onto the zipper fastening of her shirt and pulled it down, nuzzled the fabric away from the soft valley, traced the line of her bra with his tongue. "It should be the finest lace...tantalising...transparent...sinfully sexy for both of us. Wouldn't you like that?"

"Yes...." A cry...a hiss...a moan of wanting.

He lifted himself to look into her eyes; hot, melting chocolate pouring over him, into him, through him, touching him as no other woman had. "Let me express what I feel for you, Sarah. In every way I can," he pleaded. "I'll make it good for you."

"Yes..."

Her sigh of surrender relieved him of his nagging concerns and released the brake he'd forced on his own raging desires. Assured she would accept gifts that would at least give her future material security and the standing she deserved in the eyes of others, Tareq set tomorrow aside and took what he could of today, kissing her in a frenzy of passion, losing himself in the glory of her giving.

CHAPTER FOURTEEN

HER skin prickled with sensitivity as Tareq smoothed the necklace of rubies around her throat…dark red fire pulsing at her accusingly in the mirror. She had given in, cast all her principles aside in letting him do this, letting him change her into someone she barely recognised. Somehow she couldn't stop it. Her resistance melted under the desire in his eyes. She wanted to please him, wanted him to be pleased with her. Nothing else seemed to matter.

"You look magnificent," he murmured, assessing the result of his re-imaging of her in the mirror, approving what he saw. Then he bent his head to her bare shoulder, kissing it, heating the skin that leapt alive to his touch, gliding his hands down her arms in a tingling caress.

Sarah stared at her reflection, wondering who she was now, what she had become in this past week, letting him mould her to his will. In the mirror was a stunningly beautiful woman. Her wild curls had been restyled to a more dramatic shape, cut so that the fabulous ruby earrings showed to full advantage on either side of a face made up to look much more than it had before…sensual, shadowy eyes, sexy red mouth.

Her dark red gown was strapless, a fan of artful pleats covering her breasts, the gleaming satin tucking into an even deeper red velvet cummerbund that accentuated the womanly curves of her figure. The skirt billowed into a rich, luxurious fullness and rustled when she walked, making her conscious of the erotic lingerie underneath it. She felt like a courtesan, attired for her lover, yet it hadn't seemed wrong when Tareq was buying all this for her, seducing her into it with the pleasure in his eyes, with his personal involvement in everything they did.

I'll make it good for you, he'd said, but she didn't know if it was good. She only knew she had changed in becoming intimately connected to him. Their desire for each other dominated her every thought and feeling, influencing her every action, heightening her senses, drawing out needs and desires that overwhelmed any rationality.

Even now—right now—as he ran feather-light finger-tips back up her arms, she felt an urgent knot of heat in her belly, wanting more of him. Her heart was thudding so violently against her rib cage, surely he must hear it. When his hands reached her shoulders he would slide them down over the swell of her breasts and...but he turned aside to pick up the velvet cape and she stood, transfixed by the strong sexuality he stirred while he draped the heavy, satin-lined garment around her shoulders.

"Time to leave," he said, his eyes glowing with pride in her...pride in his possession?

She didn't want to go to Marchington Hall tonight, didn't want her mother to see her dressed like this. Nevertheless, she couldn't bring herself to reject what Tareq had taken so much pleasure in doing for her. Without a word, she accompanied him downstairs and out to the chauffeured Rolls-Royce which would take them on the forty-five-minute journey out of London to the stately home of the Earl of Marchester.

The car provided the same sense of private luxury as

the limousines Tareq had used in Australia and America; tinted, one-way windows, a glass panel between them and the driver, a bar with a bottle of champagne and glasses ready for them, dishes of nuts and olives, radio, disc-player.

Sarah thought whimsically of her innocent awareness of Tareq on the trip out to Werribee. Here they were, almost two months later, in a similar situation—going to visit her family—and her sexual knowledge of him made her awareness intensely pervasive as the chauffeur closed them in together.

"You're very quiet," Tareq commented. He took her hand, interlacing her fingers with his, energising the flow of feeling between them. "Are you worried about this meeting with your mother?"

He was always so quick to read her mind. Sarah wished she could read his as easily. She looked at him, trying to see through to his heart. Beyond the incredibly consuming passion they shared, she didn't know what he felt for her. His eyes were soft, kind, concerned.

"I look...too glamorous for me, Tareq."

"No. This is a you that's possible, any time you want to present it. Don't ever limit yourself, Sarah. You should feel you can belong to any world you choose."

His world? Was this dressing up a preparation for her to look appropriate in a sheikh's palace? Did he need to present her like this when he returned to his homeland for his half-brother's wedding?

"Is it better for you...politically speaking...looking as I do tonight?"

He shook his head, smiling at her reasoning. "I wanted it for you, not for me, Sarah. I think you have felt like a cuckoo for too long. Your mother won't regard you as one this evening."

He was certainly right on that score. The cuckoo had been turned into a peacock. "She'll think you've bought me," was her wry comment.

"It doesn't matter. You and I both know differently. We are only going to bridge a gap with your mother, are we not? Goodwill at Christmas? And speaking of gaps..." He lifted her hand and kissed the inner side of her wrist, making her pulse leap at the electric contact with his mouth. His eyes simmered over the sensual caress. "I wish I could bridge the one between us right now. But for rumpling that perfect dress, I would." He slid her hand down to his lap. "This I shall be feeling all night, waiting for you, wanting you."

She couldn't resist stroking her fingers along the hardness stretched so tightly against his trousers, feeling its thickness, its power, knowing she had excited it, exciting herself with thinking of how it made her feel, this extension of him seeking her, wanting connection, sinking into her innermost depths.

She forgot where they were going and her search for meaning in what he did for her. His arousal spun her along other paths of thought. Spasms of remembered ecstasy convulsed through her. She wondered if she could touch him the way he touched her, driving her mindless with ever-mounting sensation while he kept control, giving her all the pleasure. She wanted him to feel that, too, wanted to give him the sense of being utterly loved to every extreme.

A wild compulsion swept through her, gathering momentum. Before the decision was even consciously made, she was turning towards him, reaching for his zipper, pulling it down. The action jolted him. His hand came down on hers.

"Let me!" she commanded.

His hold eased. "It would mess you up, Sarah. We can't…"

"*I* can. I don't want you to touch me, Tareq. This is just for you."

For me, too, she thought fiercely. Somehow he was always taking her over. She needed to feel she was giving him something, making him feel very specially loved, every part of him special to her, loved, adored, cherished. She worked quickly to free him, her heart pumping with bursts of adrenalin.

His thighs tensed as her fingers closed around him, drawing him fully erect for her to stroke and caress and make him realise how deeply she cared for his pleasure. He had tasted her so often, turning her into a seething mass of incredible sensation. It was her turn.

He was so big it was an exciting challenge, taking him into her mouth, learning the shape of him… delicately, tentatively at first, and then more boldly, confidently. It was incredibly erotic, thinking of her red-lipsticked mouth surrounding him, circling him, imprinting him with her possession.

It was amazing, marvellous, taking him like this. And Tareq certainly wanted it. He slid forward on the seat, giving her more access, his stomach contracting, his breathing quickening. She sensed he was enraptured, his entire body focused on the sensations plunging from her mouth. She took him deeper, revelling in his excitement, exulting in the power to tease and tantalise, drawing out the exquisite anticipation, driving him to the throbbing edge of ecstasy, but not too quickly. She wanted the feelings to build and build, giving him all the delicious tingles and tension of approaching climax.

She slid a hand between his taut thighs, squeezing gently, wanting him to erupt beyond any semblance of control, wildly and wonderfully, as she did when he kissed and caressed her most intimate place.

She heard him groan. It was so good to hear that involuntary response. Her own excitement soared as he lifted himself to her, giving himself, arching for more, wanting all she gave, craving it. She felt the straining tension of his being poised on the brink, and she took him beyond it, drinking him in, loving the sense of owning him more fully, more intimately than she ever had before.

No gap between them, she thought with deep, primitive satisfaction. This made them equals. She had made him come, taking him into that incredibly blissful state all by herself. She lifted her head and looked at him, needing to see if he felt as exalted by the experience as she did.

His eyes were dark, swimming with surges of emotion. His mouth was soft, slightly parted. She saw the effort he made to recollect himself and smiled, knowing she had taken him on a journey this time, one he had not expected nor been prepared for. She had been the leader, the one initiating action, the one who took him into the sweet valley of peace, the one who gave unstintingly, asking nothing in return. It was amazing how fulfilled that made her feel as a woman...knowing she had pleasured her man to the ultimate limit.

"Thank you," he said softly, his voice deeply furred with the feelings she had evoked. "You touch me in ways I have never felt before. I have never known anyone like you."

A huge wave of emotion swelled through her, bringing tears to her eyes. "There can never be anyone like you for me, either."

He touched her cheek in a tender salute, then smiled, happiness bursting into his eyes. "I think this calls for a glass of champagne."

She laughed, lovingly watching him resettle on the seat and zip himself into proper formality again. She was deliriously happy, caught up in the thraldom of a love that knew no barriers.

"So now you don't have to wait," she bubbled, riding a high that didn't need champagne to elevate it any further.

"Oh, I'll be waiting, my sweet." His eyes sparkled wickedly at her as he lifted the bottle out of its ice bucket. "Waiting to give you a slice of heaven on the return journey. With the same rules applying. You sit. I touch."

Heaven... Sarah laughed again, excited by the prospect, loving his lust for her, exhilaratingly sure it had to encompass a love as strong as hers. And there was absolutely no reason to care what her mother thought. This designer dress meant nothing. The jewels meant nothing. What sizzled between her and Tareq was everything. They were bound together, uniquely special to each other. She was certain of it.

This conviction carried Sarah through their arrival at Marchington Hall, keeping her pleasantly detached from any sense of embarrassment over her mother's effusive greeting and the introductions that followed. There was a certain cynical amusement in hearing the unaccustomed pride in her mother's voice as she recited again and again, "My daughter, Sarah... My daughter, Sarah..." obviously brimming with pleasure in their relationship now that Sarah had the appearance of belonging to an aristocratic society, albeit through Tareq.

The cynicism turned into sadness as she reflected that her mother had never given her a sense of belonging. It was doubtful she ever would. They were poles apart in their thinking and the rift was too wide to be closed. This meeting established a token peace between them but it was empty of any real meaning.

Sarah was relieved to realise it wasn't important to her anymore. She belonged to Tareq now. She didn't need anyone else. They were together, wonderfully excitingly together. Not once did he stray from her side. Nor did he allow anyone to take her from his.

There were twenty-two guests for dinner and when they were ushered into the banquet room to take their seats for dinner, she noted all the other couples were separated, but not her and Tareq. They were seated together. As they always had been in Washington and New York.

"Did you demand that we not be parted?" she whispered as he held her chair for her.

"I stipulated it on my acceptance," he answered, his eyes warmly possessive. "The pleasure of being with you is mine."

It made her feel even more loved and wanted.

This was not the first time Sarah had dined in the banquet room at Marchington Hall with all the splendours of centuries of wealth surrounding her; a magnificent hand-painted ceiling set in ornate plasterwork, dazzling chandeliers, silk curtains luxuriously draped to pool on the highly polished parquet floor, huge gilt mirrors, marble fireplaces, paintings by masters that would have been coveted by any museum, Chippendale furniture, and on the long, mirror-like surface of the table, the finest Spode china, gleaming silver cutlery, and exquisitely cut Baccarat crystal. It *was*, however, the first time she didn't feel like a total alien here.

She had always thought such wealth obscene.

Yet what it provided *was* beautiful, a feast of riches that seduced the senses. And having put herself in Tareq's hands, Sarah had succumbed to it, accepting all he wanted her to accept. *I'll make it good for you*, he'd said, and she now decided he had. Even this. With him at her side, colouring it all with intense happiness, sharing, involved, he made her feel she could, indeed, walk into any world and belong. Somehow he had completely refocused her life.

She looked down the table to where her mother sat at the foot of it, holding court to those sitting closest to her...the countess...and Sarah could see, and finally acknowledge how brilliantly she suited the role. It still saddened her that she had virtually been locked out of her mother's life, that their values were so different, but she wondered if she had been too judgmental, too critical. What did she really know of her mother's innermost feelings?

Michael Kearney could have been as overwhelming as Tareq. In which case, it would have been devastating to lose him to another woman. The earl was certainly a good deal older, but if he made her mother feel good about herself, and she gave him what he wanted, perhaps there was more to the marriage than money and position.

Sarah knew her mother to be forty-eight though she

barely looked thirty, her gleaming blonde hair softly styled to enhance a prettiness kept young by skilful nips and tucks. She was dressed in a slim, elegant silver gown, diamonds at her throat and ears, all especially chosen, Sarah thought, to echo the lovely groups of angels set on the table as Christmas decorations.

In years gone by, she had viewed her mother's obsession with perfect detail—superficial detail—with secret contempt, turning away from it, resenting the time given to it, despising the kind of values it represented. People were more important than having things look right.

Yet there was pleasure in it, pleasure and satisfaction.

Her mother glanced down the table, caught Sarah's gaze, and smiled, delight and warm pleasure lighting her face.

Sarah couldn't help smiling back. She felt good. She felt beautiful. She felt loved. And it was Christmas Eve, a time for peace and goodwill. She was glad that her mother felt happy, even if it was brought about by superficial things that didn't really matter.

The food and wine were superb, or maybe everything just tasted better because sitting with Tareq sharpened all her senses. Occasionally he grazed her hand with his fingertips. Daringly, she scraped her nails along his thigh. He blew softly in her ear, pretending some confidential murmur. She lifted her glass of wine, her eyes promising a different toast to the one she mouthed. It was a delicious game.

She noticed the smudge of red from her lower lip on her crystal wineglass and thought of the ring of red she might have left on him, then almost squirmed in excited anticipation of what he was going to do to her on the return trip to London. *You sit. I touch.* All the possibilities of how he would touch danced through her mind.

The dinner conversation around them seemed like a lot of distant yapping, not affecting them even when out of politeness they had to respond. They shared an intense private world, their bodies humming to the same tune, their eyes secretly feasting on far more than what was set on the table.

Coffee was served in the drawing room. Knowing that Tareq would soon call for the car—the urgent hunger burning in his eyes was warning enough he wouldn't wait much longer—Sarah excused herself to take advantage of the powder room before they left.

Her mother waylaid her, hooking her arm around Sarah's. "Darling, come upstairs with me. We can repair our make-up together and have a little chat."

Sarah inwardly recoiled from the "little chat" suggestion. Any distraction from Tareq was unwelcome, especially the kind of frivolous conversation her mother indulged in. She wanted to hurry back to him. He was waiting for her.

But her mother beamed at her expectantly and Sarah's conscience was pricked by daughterly duty. It had been two years. It was Christmas. And a few minutes of inconsequential chatter shouldn't feel such an unwanted burden, shouldn't stir such tense frustration.

Just a few minutes of being civil...

No matter what her mother said, it wouldn't change anything between her and Tareq.

CHAPTER FIFTEEN

"I CAN'T get over how wonderful you look!" her mother gushed, drawing her along to the staircase. "You're absolutely glowing."

"Thank you, Mother. You look wonderful, too. It's been a lovely evening."

The arm around hers hugged more tightly, her mother leaning closer, conspiratorially. "Those rubies are fabulous. They must have cost a fortune."

Sarah cringed at the avid note in her voice. "I really have no idea what they're worth," she said flatly. "Tareq bought them."

Soft, indulgent laughter. "He's obviously besotted with you. I must say you surprised me, linking up with him. Oh, I know he's stunningly handsome and terribly sexy, but you were always such a stickler for love and marriage."

Sarah kept her mouth firmly shut, glancing up to the next floor and wishing there were fewer stairs to climb.

"I suppose he swept you off your feet and offered you the earth. And I must say he's being very generous. Those rubies are fabulous. Has he given you any other jewellery?"

Sarah gritted her teeth. She hated this. "Mother, I'm with Tareq because I love him," she bit out.

"Well, of course you do, dear." Another arm squeeze. "But you must know it won't last with him. It's not as if he'd ever marry you."

Sarah flinched. She hadn't thought that far, but if they loved each other, wasn't marriage the natural progression? She couldn't imagine life without Tareq.

"You don't understand, Mother," she said tersely.

"Sarah, you can't imagine he'll marry you," came the incredulous retort. "Tareq al-Khaima is a sheikh. As English as he might seem to be, his own culture will eventually claim him. You have your head in the clouds if you think anything else, believe me."

Nothing and nobody dictates to Tareq how to live his life. He had told her so himself. Sarah clung grimly to that thought as they reached the head of the stairs and turned towards the first guest suite. She was not going to argue with her mother. There was no point to it.

Her silence, however, was a goad. "My dear, he may seem to be free-wheeling, but when it comes to marriage, he'll do what he thinks is best for his country and that won't be you."

She was wrong. Tareq wasn't going to fall in with his uncle's wishes.

When the well-meant advice met with no response, her mother's reasonableness sharpened to exasperation. "The hard truth is you're the latest in a long line of women who've come and gone in Tareq al-Khaima's life. He has the reputation of being very generous while they're with him. That's the way the game is played, Sarah."

"It might have been with them. It won't be with me," she fiercely stated, hating the imputation and refusing to let in any doubt. So he liked buying women things. He liked being generous. It didn't mean he thought of her as he had his previous lovers.

"Oh, Sarah..." Her mother shook her head despairingly as she opened the door to the suite and waved Sarah inside. ''What makes you think you're any different?''

Because she was. Tareq had told her so. No other woman touched him the way she did. He'd never known anyone like her before. But her mother would probably scorn such avowals as nothing more than a lover's flattery, spoiling the special feeling with her horrid view of Tareq's interest in her.

''Please excuse me, Mother. I need to use the bathroom.'' She crossed the bedroom quickly, heading for the bathroom door.

''If he was really serious about you, Sarah, and not playing the usual game, why do you suppose he bought you those rubies?''

The hard question knifed her heart and left it quivering. She kept going, denying her mother the satisfaction of thinking she'd scored a hit. The problem was, she could shut the bathroom door on her mother but she couldn't shut out her thoughts.

Why had Tareq insisted on buying her things, pressing her to take them, seducing her into accepting them? She'd told him she didn't want them. He'd overridden her protest. Was it because he didn't like to leave her with nothing…when they parted?

No…no…she wasn't going to believe that. He had explained his motives and they were good, caring, wanting her to feel confident.

Then why had she felt like a courtesan earlier tonight?

Stop it! she screamed at herself. Remember how it had been in the car coming here. He loved her. He really truly loved her. It was stupid to let her mother—her mother, of all people—put doubts in her mind. She'd known all along her mother would think Tareq had bought her.

He was waiting for her and he loved her and the sooner she got back to him the better.

Determinedly she carried on with using the bathroom facilities, wishing she could recapture the excitement her mother had stolen with her insidious comments. All the lovely anticipation was gone. But surely it would come back once she was with Tareq again. He'd look at her and she'd know their togetherness was rock-solid. He'd draw her back into their private world and everything would be all right.

Having shored up her confidence, Sarah left the bathroom, intent on making a quick escape downstairs. Her mother was agitatedly pacing the floor, back and forth across the path to the bedroom door, frustrating an easy exit. She fastened a pained but resolute gaze on her daughter.

"Sarah...for your own good, this is one time when you must listen to me."

"Mother, please leave it. Tareq is waiting..."

"No! You can give me a few more minutes of your time. It's not asking much."

Reluctant to completely snub her mother, Sarah stood mutinously silent, mentally blocking her ears, determined on not letting anything that was said unsettle her further.

The pacing continued, accompanied by vehement gestures, emphasising the bewilderment and frustration behind the outpouring of words. "I know you don't think much of it, but I have tried to do my best by you, Sarah. You've always made it very difficult. You never forgave me for leaving your father, yet the truth was we weren't happy together. We were mismatched. He never wanted to do the things I wanted to do…"

"Mother, that's way in the past," Sarah cut in impatiently.

She was ignored. "You were barely civil to Michael and you always looked at me with accusing eyes. I wanted to be happy. Maybe that was selfish of me. Whatever… The best solution seemed to be to send you to boarding school."

Out of sight, out of mind, Sarah thought.

Her mother raved on. "I chose that school carefully for you, Sarah, wanting you to make the social connections that would help give you a good start in life. You seemed to take pleasure in defeating my purpose."

Sarah grimaced at the lack of understanding. "It didn't work that way, Mother. The other girls saw no profit in knowing me."

"You didn't try!" came the angry retaliation. "You didn't try anything I lined up for you. You just turned up your nose at everything. Even the eligible men I introduced you to."

"They were wrong for me."

"And you think Sheikh Tareq al-Khaima is right?" A scathing whiplash. "I don't know what goes on in your mind, Sarah. All your decisions seem to be self-defeating. Now you're blindly involving yourself with a man who could at least do something for you if you played your cards sensibly. He would probably give you…"

"Don't start on Tareq again," Sarah cut in, hard and fast, her stomach cramping in instant revulsion for any mercenary conversation targeting the man she loved.

Her mother would not be stopped. "What you're

thinking is so foolish, and all you'll end up with is a broken heart.''

"So be it then," Sarah sliced in, determined on cutting her short.

"Just listen to yourself! So impossibly stubborn. Closing your eyes to obvious realities. I don't know how long you've been lovers, but in all that time, has he ever once said he loves you?''

Tareq hadn't actually said it in words but that didn't make any difference. He did love her. She knew it. He was waiting for her so he could show how much he loved her again and again and again!

Although a disquietening little memory did niggle...her asking Tareq if he'd lost the capacity to love...his replying it had been whittled away. And even then he'd wanted her, waiting until she was willing. Willing...

A chill crawled down her spine. Her hand crept up and tugged at the ruby necklace. It felt uncomfortable around her throat.

"So he hasn't declared his love," her mother concluded, having waited for an answer that hadn't come.

There was no triumph in her voice. The words were spoken in a dead tone, empty of hope and not expecting any. Sarah wanted to defy the knowingness in her mother's eyes. The sadness and sympathy shining through the knowingness made it even worse...hurting because the understanding was wrong.

Her mother sighed, then pushed another *destroy* button. "Has he talked about the future with you?"

Defensively Sarah clutched at the known fact that Tareq certainly had a year with her in mind. There was plenty of time ahead to start looking beyond that. And it was perfectly possible she had stirred the capacity to love in him. She didn't want these doubts. They hurt. They twisted things.

"Sarah, has he actually promised you anything?" her mother pressed, relentless in forcing the issue.

I never make promises I don't intend to keep.

She frowned. It was too soon for promises anyway. They'd only been lovers for ten days. She was *not* going to think about it. Her mother was judging on things that had nothing to do with what was really going on between her and Tareq. She wouldn't listen to any more.

"No talk of love or the future and no promises made," her mother recited, hammering home what she saw as damning facts. "Now will you listen to sense?"

"No." A violent revulsion rose out of the sick churning. "Not your kind of sense, Mother. You've laid it out for me. You've done your best. I'm sorry I don't appreciate it more but I'd rather go my own way. Thank you and goodnight."

She moved quickly, deftly skirting her mother as she headed for the door.

"Sarah, I am trying to help," came the last urgent plea.

She paused, her hand on the knob, desperate to get away from the constant clawing at her heart, yet tugged into one last reply by what had probably been a genuine desire to help, regardless of its miserable outcome. She glanced back.

"I'm sorry, Mother. Please forgive my shortcomings and have a happy Christmas. I do have to go now. Tareq is waiting for me."

She left, but there was no joy in the going, no sense of happy anticipation winging her steps down the staircase. Her mind was a jangle of unresolved questions. Her chest felt so tight it was painful to breathe. Her soul screamed that she had to have faith…faith and trust. Tareq set a lot of store in trust. Absolute trust.

Then she saw him. Her feet faltered. He was at the end of the great hall, speaking to the butler. Was their car outside waiting? Waiting to enclose them in fevered intimacy again? Her heart pounded so hard all her pulse points throbbed. She wasn't just another one of his women. She wasn't!

He turned and saw her. She watched him come to the foot of the staircase, strong, purposeful, so very sure of where he was going and what he would do. *I always try to balance what I give and take, Sarah. I pride myself on playing fair.* He'd taken her gift of pleasuring him and now he was going to give it back. Playing fair. But what did the rubies mean…by the rules he'd set himself?

He held out his hand to her, his eyes drawing her down to him like a magnet, telling her she was mesmerisingly beautiful, infinitely desirable, and no other woman could hold a candle to her. The wanting to be with her—only with her—pulsed from him and squeezed her heart.

But did he love her?

Would he always love her?

The wretched doubts swirled around her like the black funnel of a tornado. There was his hand held out to her, an offering of himself, unwavering, an open invitation to the togetherness she craved, compelling her to take it. With a sense of inevitability, she laid her own hand in his.

What else could she do?
She loved him.
He was her world.

CHAPTER SIXTEEN

CHRISTMAS morning…a crisp, fine day…and two clear weeks at the estate in Surrey ahead of them. Tareq revelled in a happiness he had never expected to feel. Even driving his Jaguar—the power, the speed, at his control—added to an exhilarating sense of freedom.

For the next fortnight he wasn't going to think of who he was or the demands of the role he'd been born to. Certainly his mother wouldn't remind him. She preferred to forget *that other life* when she was married to his father. Christmas Day would be very English, the rest of their stay with her, likewise. She wouldn't dream of intruding on his relationship with Sarah. Acceptance with grace and discretion was assured.

Besides, his mother excelled in providing a cosy, comfortable atmosphere. Sarah would like Hershaw Manor. It was much more of a home than the very stately, impersonal Marchington Hall. He wanted her to feel at home. Christmas tended to tug at family strings and she could be missing what she'd shared with Jessie and the twins on the two Christmas days she'd spent in Australia. Was being with him enough for her?

"What are you thinking?" he asked, suddenly craving a reconnection with her mind. It was almost obsessive, the desire to possess all of her. She was like a compelling narcotic. He kept wanting more and more and more.

He felt her glance at him, sensed her reluctance to reveal her thoughts, and the determination to know them impelled him to reach over and take her hand, using touch to forge the intimate mood that encouraged confidences. "Tell me," he softly urged.

She sighed. "I was wondering what your mother would think of us."

He flashed her a reassuring smile. "She'll think you're very lovely and I'm very lucky to have you."

She remained pensive, distant from him. "Have you taken other women with you to Hershaw Manor, Tareq?"

He frowned, not liking the comparison she was toying with, not liking the strained note in her voice. Still, he could not lie to her. "Yes, I have." He squeezed her hand. "But none like you, Sarah."

She looked down, her gaze fastening on the physical link he was pressing. "Will your mother know that?" she asked quietly. "Or will she think I'm just another bit of...of passing trade?"

The phrase thumped into Tareq's heart, making him wince at the crass impact it carried. He'd had many pleasurable interludes with women but he hadn't *bought* them. All his previous liaisons had been mutually agreeable. As this one was. To use the word *trade*...he flinched from it.

"I've never consorted with whores," he said gruffly. "And my mother certainly wouldn't consider you one." He threw her a critical look. "Why are you thinking in such offensive terms?"

She evaded eye contact, turning her head towards the side window of the car. He saw only the hotly flushed skin of her neck and cheek.

"I'm sorry," she said in a small voice. "I didn't mean

to offend you. I was just wondering…where I'd stand in your mother's eyes. It is for two weeks…''

Vulnerable! The realisation of how she was feeling jolted him. He'd forgotten she lacked the experience and sophistication to feel at ease with his mother's knowing and accommodating the fact of their being lovers. He took his mother's acceptance for granted. How could Sarah take anything for granted, not knowing, not even having been in such a situation before? She was no longer an innocent sexually but she was still very much an innocent at heart…open to giving and open to being hurt.

Damn it! He should never have started this. All the justification in the world didn't make it right. Not for her. He couldn't balance what he'd taken. Yet if he had the chance to turn back the clock and give up what she'd given him…no, he needed this, needed to have and know these incredibly rare feelings at least once in his lifetime. And she was experiencing them, too. It might never happen again for her, either. They had to seize as much as they could while they could.

He retrieved his hand in order to change gear, slow the car, park on the verge of the road.

"What's wrong?" she cried, swinging her head back to him in alarm at the abrupt action.

"You are," he said, switching off the engine.

"Tareq…please forget what I said," she rushed out in a fluster. "It doesn't matter. I was being…"

He placed a gentle, silencing finger on her lips. "I want you to know how special you are, Sarah. You see, my darling girl…" He hoped she could see it in his eyes, feel it flowing from him. He cupped her face to hold her still, hold her tied to him while he said what he had to impress on her. "...I love being with you. I love everything about you. I love you so much my mother can't fail to see it. And she will look at you in wonder because I've never loved anyone else. So you have nothing to fear from her. There will be no awkwardness. Only happiness, my love."

He felt his heart turn over at the luminous look of joy in her eyes. Never mind that they were on a public road. He leaned over and kissed her, loving the way her mouth seemed to melt into his, loving her passion, loving the giving that poured into all the empty places in his heart and refreshed his soul.

"I love you, too, Tareq," she whispered when they'd drunk their fill of each other.

He smiled, knowing it couldn't be anything else but true, coming from Sarah. "Then that's where we stand," he said. "Are you okay with it now?"

She laughed, exhilaration sparkling in her eyes. "Yes. Very okay, thank you."

He laughed with her. It was so good. It was as if everything within him was humming with happiness. When he restarted the Jaguar, he couldn't resist a burst of acceleration.

Two uninterrupted weeks of bliss, he thought exultantly, as they sped towards Hershaw Manor. After that...he didn't want to think about it...although one thing he had to find out was what Sarah would like to do in the future. He felt a deep twinge of regret at the necessity to provide some foundation for her to build on. Realities, however, could not be pushed into the background forever.

There had to be something he could arrange by way of settling Sarah into an occupation or career she would find rewarding. He had the power to open doors, make useful introductions, finance anything she wanted.

People were lost without a purpose in life.

He would make absolutely sure Sarah had something of substance to work with, to carry her forward, to give her satisfaction and fulfilment as a person. She had the inner strength of a survivor but he wanted more than survival for her.

He wished he could give her everything.

CHAPTER SEVENTEEN

SARAH loved Hershaw Manor. It was as warm and welcoming as Tareq's mother. The rooms were chock-a-block with personality; pretty chintz fabrics used in most of the furnishings, patterned carpets, a huge collection of antiques from different periods, chosen for charm and character rather than style, and every possession seemed to have a memory attached to it.

There were horses in the stables for riding, dogs underfoot, as much part of the household as people, and a casual, country mood imbued the life that flowed in and out and through the lovely old building in its parkland setting.

Tareq's mother—"Do call me Penny, dear. Everyone does."—Penelope Lambert—had married again to a veterinary surgeon, and had been widowed a few years ago. In her fifties now, she still had a wonderful vivacity that lit up the beauty of her youth, especially her sparkling blue eyes and beautiful smile. Her thick wavy hair was unashamedly white, though it had once been a glorious, rich red, as evidenced in many framed photographs of her with the champion Corgis she bred.

Kindness oozed from her. It was from her Tareq had learned his kindness, Sarah thought, and wondered if his father had been ruthless. Where did inherited genes begin and end and where did conditioning take over? Impossible to tell. She remembered her impression there was always purpose in Tareq's kindness and decided it wasn't necessarily so.

Though she did have an uncertain moment or two one evening. She and Penny shared an interest in books, both of them being avid readers.

"Have you ever tried to write one?" Penny asked.

"No. Have you?"

"I dabble with the occasional article about dogs. It's fun, playing with words, getting them in the right order so they shape the picture you want to draw. Like doing a jigsaw."

Sarah was amused by the parallel. "I'd love to read what you've had published. Actually it's the publishing side of books that interests me. I imagine it could be very exciting being an editor, getting a great manuscript and helping to turn it into a book people will want to buy."

"Do you have any first-hand knowledge of the publishing business?" Tareq asked, suddenly showing a keen interest in the conversation.

"Not really. I just think the whole process would be fascinating. Not only getting the book right for print but planning the cover and the selling points."

"We don't have any investment in that area," he said thoughtfully. "I'll look into it. Publishing must be profitable."

"Don't you have enough business to control already?" she teased.

He smiled. "I was thinking more along the lines of appointing you manager."

"Oh, don't be silly! I wouldn't have a clue."

"Think of the challenge."

"You're not serious."

"I think it's a splendid idea!" Penny interjected. "Just think, Sarah. Tareq could fix it for you to learn every aspect of the business first and then you could produce a lovely line of books." Her beautiful smile lit up her face. "Of course, I'd expect free copies."

"It's only a pipedream I had," Sarah protested, embarrassed that it had been seized upon by both of them.

"Let him spoil you. That's what men are for," Penny airily declared. "I've got my dogs. You should have your books."

Tareq grinned. "Thank you, Mother."

Kindness, generosity… Tareq insisted he loved her and wanted her to be happy…but Sarah didn't see how she could pursue a career, however attractive, and be with him, too. He travelled so much. Surely he wouldn't want to leave her behind.

Or was he looking at a future when they wouldn't be together anymore?

Kindness with a purpose.

She pushed the unsettling idea into the background, blaming her own mother for raising that spectre. Tareq's motive could just as easily be precisely what he said, not wanting her to get bored or restless, doing nothing of any consequence. Though she wouldn't be doing nothing if they got married and had children.

Deciding to let the future look after itself, she immersed herself in the joy of each wonderful day at the manor. She loved being here with Tareq. He seemed softer somehow, more relaxed, more open to her in this place that had been home to him through most of his growing up years. His mother had the habit of drawing out his sense of humour, adding fun to the pleasure of getting to know him better.

They rode most mornings, walked the dogs in the afternoon, helped his mother with a huge jigsaw—she was addicted to them—which accounted for a certain pattern in Tareq's thinking—enjoyed cosy little parties with local friends, played cards, spent many hours lounging by the fire in the sitting room, idly conversing, and many more hours making love in the privacy of their bedroom.

To Sarah it was an idyllic existence. She hoped the closeness they'd forged here would be carried on when they left. But her hopes and dreams received a shattering blow the day before she and Tareq were to return to London.

She was helping Penny do some more of her giant jigsaw while Tareq was busy with telephone calls. She couldn't help grinning triumphantly as she fitted in a piece they'd all been searching for over the past week. "There!" she cried, and they both laughed.

Penny sat back, shaking her head in a bemused fashion. "You remind me so much of myself with Tareq's father. The heady days of passion...so impossible to believe we couldn't overcome everything with our love."

Sadness dulled her eyes and Sarah was prompted to ask, "Why did it end, Penny?"

She shrugged and gave a rueful smile. "His country claimed him. I didn't fit in there. The culture was so different. I was always viewed as *the foreigner* by those closest to him, pushed into the background. And passion fades when love doesn't overcome everything."

"I'm sorry," Sarah murmured sympathetically, wondering if she would face the same problems, then quickly assuring herself times had changed. Thirty years ago, countries were much more insular than they were now.

"Oh, I don't regret having known such passion even though it didn't last. Seeing you and Tareq so wonderfully consumed by it... I'm glad for both of you. It's rather rare, you know. It's worth having, every minute of it."

Sarah smiled, her happiness brimming over.

"There was nothing like it in my second marriage," Penny went on. "It was...comforting...congenial. We had a great deal in common and sharing is nice."

Nice...such a weak, insipid word.

"It's especially nice when the only sharing you've done for years was in bed," Penny added wryly.

Sarah felt a twinge of apprehension about how much sharing there'd be with Tareq once they left here. He'd be back to business with Peter Larsen, then the trip to his homeland for the wedding. Claims on him would certainly be made there. Their time together would be quality time, Sarah decided, deep, glorious quality time.

"Sarah..." A pained look had come into Penny's eyes. "Maybe I shouldn't say this. It's really none of my business. But...I've come to care about you and...and I feel you believe everything is possible for you and Tareq..."

"Yes, I do," Sarah affirmed, trying to ignore a prickling of alarm.

Penny shook her head in some anguish of spirit. "You'll be so terribly hurt...if you're not prepared."

The prickling turned into a nasty crawl down her spine. She had been through this scene before. With her mother. Though surely it couldn't be the same. Tareq's mother had seen they loved each other. There had to be something else on her mind.

"What do you mean?" Sarah asked warily, trying to fight off the anxiety attacking her heart.

A deep breath. A look that appealed for both forgiveness and understanding. "Don't bank on this lasting, Sarah...what you have with Tareq now."

No...please don't say that. Please?

The words kept coming. "There's too much against your staying together for very long."

We're strong enough to beat any problems.

"The time will come when you'll have to let it go," came the unequivocal statement. Blue eyes—so like Tareq's—begging belief. "Just...be prepared for that time, my dear."

It was said so kindly, Sarah found she couldn't dismiss the advice as she had her own mother's, however much she wanted to. This woman knew her son, knew more about him than any outsider could ever know, except perhaps Peter Larsen whose loyalty to Tareq would forbid him giving any advice that might be against his friend's interests.

"Why..." She swallowed, then forced out the question. "Why are you so sure it can't last?"

A heavy sigh, then slowly, agonisingly, a list of cogent reasons. "This is not a simple life you're dealing with. A marriage between you and Tareq would be a disaster. A half-English sheikh is barely acceptable to his people. Taking a wife, not of his country, would destabilise Tareq's authority. As much as he might want to force his will on the situation, there are those who would work against him. And you, Sarah, would be caught in the middle of it."

Tareq had actually spelled it out to her when they were leaving Werribee. It seemed like aeons ago, but the truth hadn't changed. His uncle…pressing him to marry a suitable woman to cement his position. Not an old man entrenched in old ways but a shrewd politician spelling out a necessity. That was what Penny was telling her, and buck as Tareq had against his uncle's choice of bride for him, the reality of the situation did not allow for Sarah to step into the role. She could only be a symbol of rebellion.

And Tareq had meant to use her as precisely that, perhaps as a staying tactic while he negotiated something else. He had anticipated their becoming lovers—no need for pretence—but had he anticipated falling in love with her? Wanting her as he did now? It made a difference, didn't it?

"Love doesn't always find a way," Penny said regretfully, as though reading the anguished hope in Sarah's mind. "It wears thin under tensions and conflict and conspiracies. Then it becomes untenable. Believe me. I know. Just…be prepared to let it go, Sarah. For your sake and his."

"But Tareq loves me." The protest burst from her heart. "He won't want to let me go, Penny."

"I can't imagine he will want to. There's the pity of it. But he knows such a journey is paved with trouble. And because he does love you, Sarah, I don't think he'll want to take you with him down that road. It would be destructive…to both of you."

Was it true? Couldn't there be some way around it? Or was he already preparing to let her go? Her frantic mind circled and fastened on the career he seemed so intent on her having. She desperately wanted to reject what it might mean, yet felt driven to face what had to be faced now. Even the worst.

"Is this why he's latched onto the idea of a publishing business for me?" she asked, her heart sinking as she saw the answer in his mother's eyes.

"I think so." Her own love for her son threaded the sadness in her voice as she explained, "Tareq has always tried to balance everything, even when it was impossible. I think he needs to find a gift for what you've given him...when the inevitable can no longer be held back."

Tears blurred Sarah's eyes. Tareq's rules...by which he could live with himself...trying to be fair. "I love him," she said helplessly.

"I know." Tears shone in Penny's eyes, too. "If I were you, I'd hoard every golden moment you have with him, Sarah. Savour every special feeling. Life with anyone you love can be so short. Don't waste it. It's worth too much to waste."

No guarantee with Tareq...only risk. Sarah recalled thinking that just after she had agreed to his bargain. After she had declared the bargain null and void, he'd asked if she'd stay with him of her own free will. She'd risked her heart, without guarantees, and the answer she'd given then was still the answer she'd give now.

Yes.

She'd stay with him until the journey ended, wherever it did, whenever it did. And she wouldn't waste a second of it.

CHAPTER EIGHTEEN

SARAH sat in the private courtyard adjoining Tareq's apartment in the palace, watching the fountain endlessly recycling water in a harmonious pattern. Fountains were supposed to be refreshing and soothing. This one was not fulfilling its purpose today. She kept wondering if Tareq was fulfilling his purpose in bringing her to his country or whether his stand was being frayed by a growing bank of opposition. Either way, she felt she was living every hour on the desperate edge of time running out on them.

She'd seen so little of him since they'd arrived a week ago. It seemed that as the ruling sheikh, his presence was required elsewhere virtually from dawn to so late at night, Sarah was sometimes asleep when he joined her in bed. She instantly awoke but he didn't want to talk about the meetings that had occupied his day. He wanted to hold her close to him.

She sensed urgent need in his lovemaking. The tensions he brought to bed with him were translated into intense passion, and only when that was sated did he relax and go to sleep, comforted by the lingering warmth of their intimate togetherness. Sarah couldn't help thinking he was being strongly pressured to set her aside. The echo of her own secret desperation seemed to vibrate in every kiss, in every possessive embrace, in the compulsive hunger for every expression of love.

Sometimes she was tempted to ask him to confide the

conflicts he faced, wanting to know the worst, yet she shied from doing anything that might precipitate the end of their being together. Love kept her tied to him for as long as he didn't actively reject it. Love...and a grain of hope for a resolution that didn't involve their parting. Though it seemed less and less feasible with every day that passed.

Adding to the despair she tried to suppress was the first-hand experience of the problems Penny Lambert had outlined to her. She was not welcome here. Tareq's stepmother and her daughters had invited her to lunch with them—only once—more to scrutinise her than to ease an entry into the family circle. Although she was treated with studied courtesy, they made her feel very foreign to them. A curiosity. An alien.

Mindful of filling in the hours for her, Tareq had arranged a guide to show her through the palace, explaining the history of its architecture and art works. She'd also been taken on tours of the city and the nearby resort on the shores of the Red Sea. The people, the places...everything was stamped with a culture so foreign to her, Sarah seriously doubted she could ever fit into it, let alone be happy living here on a permanent basis, despite being domiciled with every luxury and servants on hand to do her bidding.

The wretched truth was...the situation was hopeless in any long-term sense. Maybe Tareq wanted her to recognise that herself before the axe fell. There needn't be only one purpose in bringing her here.

"Sarah..." Tareq calling her.

Amazed at his seeking her out midmorning, she leapt up from the garden seat to be more easily seen. "I'm out here."

He strode through the archway to the courtyard, his sheikh's robes somehow giving him more stature, while clothing him in an unfamiliarity that subtly emphasised how little Sarah had comprehended the full nature of this man she loved. Nevertheless, there was a huge grin on his face and his obvious good humour lifted Sarah's heart.

"Come…" He beckoned expansively. "…I have a surprise for you."

A surge of happiness sped her feet towards him. The fact that Tareq was here to spend some time with her was delight enough. He glanced back over his shoulder, nodding to someone in the shadows of the salon beyond the arches. Sarah looked past him to see what the surprise might be.

A red and yellow wheelchair came zooming into the sunlight and a high excited voice cried, "It's me, Sarah!"

"Jessie!"

Hugs and kisses and emotional tears and words tumbling over each other…

"It's so wonderful to see you."

"Tareq had me flown here in his private jet."

"All this way on your own?"

"A nurse came with me. And Peter was at the airport to pick us up."

"You mean Mr. Larsen?"

"He said I can call him Peter. And I've got special rooms in the palace with all the stuff I need."

"Truly?"

"Peter showed me. I'm to stay for the wedding so I'll see all the sheikhs."

"Oh, that's marvellous, Jessie! I'm so happy to have you here with me."

"Me, too. Doesn't Tareq look terrific in his robes?"

"He looks terrific to me whatever he wears."

"Or don't wear," Tareq muttered wickedly.

They laughed, Jessie not quite understanding but bubbling with so much excitement it didn't matter what they laughed at. The next few hours skimmed by, the pleasure of catching up with each other's news enhanced by Tareq's staying with them and light-heartedly stirring more fun with his dry sense of humour.

They had a lovely lunch together. When Jessie started to flag, Sarah and Tareq accompanied her to the specially prepared suite of rooms where she happily crowed over her new domain and introduced the nurse who had been employed to look after her, a cheerful woman in her thirties who seemed to be enjoying this adventure as much as Jessie. She steered her young charge into getting ready for an afternoon nap, leaving Sarah and Tareq alone together in the sitting room while she was settling Jessie into bed.

"It was so kind of you to do this," Sarah murmured, turning to him, her eyes eloquently expressing a heart full of love.

His arms came around her in an ardent embrace. "You've been lonely here," he answered gruffly. "It was selfish of me to bring you with me, but there was need, Sarah. I hope having Jessie's company will make it easier for you."

Need...the word buzzed through her brain, stirring a maelstrom of hopes and doubts. "Have I helped? With your uncle, I mean," she rushed out, searching his eyes for answers.

"Your presence reinforces my decisions," he said enigmatically.

"Is it...difficult for you?"

His face relaxed into a wry smile. "Yes and no." He lifted a hand to her cheek and tenderly fanned her skin with his fingertips. "As much as one might be determined on change, there is an underlying tug for what has been in place, for what is so ingrained it becomes a part of natural thought."

She sensed the inner torment of a struggle that tore him in two and knew intuitively it was centred on her. "Will you explain that to me?" she pleaded, suddenly uncaring of the outcome for her, wanting him to share his pain as well as his love.

He shook his head. "The problem is mine, my darling. And it's up to me to overcome it. Can you bear with me for a while longer?"

"You know I will," she cried fervently. "As long as you want me."

The wanting blazed into his eyes and seared her mouth as he kissed her, drawing from her all she would give and demanding more, hotly and hungrily, wanting so much it felt as though he was absorbing the very essence of her being, plundering her of energy to reinforce his own for the battle he was fighting.

A loud, theatrical cough broke the torrent of passion. Dizzily, Sarah heard the nurse say, "Uh, please pardon me...it's Jessie. She's in bed but she wants to tell you something before you...um...leave about your business."

Tareq took a deep breath. "Fine. Thank you," he said with creditable aplomb.

He scooped Sarah along with him to Jessie's bedroom

and the nurse scuttled out of their way, retreating to her own adjoining quarters in a flood of embarrassment at having witnessed and interrupted the sheikh's dalliance with what should have been very private desires.

Jessie was watching for them to come in, her gaze latching onto Tareq as they walked over to her bed. "I forgot to say thank you for bringing me here."

"I wanted it, Jessie," he confided. "I'm glad you were brave enough to make the trip."

She grinned. "Wild horses wouldn't have stopped me. I'm going to brag about this for years."

"Then you must tell me everything you want to do and see while you're my guest."

She heaved a big sigh. "You've been so good to me already with the computer and all. Mummy said Sarah must have told you about Firefly and that was why you wanted to do things for me."

Sarah shook her head but her little half-sister had all her attention focused on Tareq.

"I don't want you to think it was Firefly's fault that my legs don't work anymore, Tareq," she said earnestly. "You don't have to make it up to me."

He frowned, inadvertantly sparking Jessie to say more.

"I don't blame him at all. Firefly got frightened by the sparkler. I just wanted to show him but it scared him real bad. He didn't know he was hurting me. I think he was trying to put the sparkler out."

Sarah's chest tightened as Jessie spilled out the cause of a painful train of events that had led to her father cheating Tareq. The reason to hide it was gone—her father had his second chance—yet it still might leave an impression of carelessness on Tareq. He looked deeply concerned as he sat down on the edge of the bed and took Jessie's hand, fondling it sympathetically.

"Why don't you tell me your story of what happened?" he invited, his tone softly persuasive.

Sarah resigned herself to the inevitable. It was out of her hands. In fact, everything was out of her hands. Tareq was the dominant force, as he had been from the very beginning.

Jessie took a deep breath and poured out the tragic little story. "It was my birthday, you see. I was eight. Mummy was in hospital having the cancer treatment that made her sick, but Mrs. Walsh—she's married to Daddy's foreman—made me a cake—a big cream sponge cake with strawberries and candles on it—and me and the twins had a party after school. We had sparklers and balloons and party hats and blow-out whistles."

"Sounds like great fun," Tareq popped in encouragingly.

"Oh, it was! But the twins tore off together, doing their twin thing…" She grimaced as though Tareq would understand what she meant. "…And I thought I'd take Firefly a big slice of my cake and share my birthday party with him."

"With a horse?" Tareq gently teased.

"Firefly isn't just any horse. He's the most beautiful horse in the world. He used to let me pat him 'cause he knew I loved him. And I often went and talked to him in his stall. I knew by his eyes he was listening and he'd nod at me."

"Yes, he does have very intelligent eyes," Tareq agreed.

A heavy sigh. "I knew I wasn't supposed to go into

his stall. Daddy said it wasn't allowed. But it was my birthday, and I thought if I sneaked in, nobody would see me but Firefly and he wouldn't tell. So I did. And you should have seen Firefly scoff the cake I'd brought him. He thought it was great."

"I'm sure he did," Tareq warmly agreed.

"But then I lit the sparkler and…like I said…it scared him. He reared up and got all frantic. I tried to calm him down but he accidentally knocked me against the wall and…" She shook her head and shrugged off the crippling injuries she'd sustained. "…I don't remember anything after that until I woke up in hospital."

"I guess it wasn't much fun in hospital."

Jessie rolled her eyes expressively. "The pits! Especially all the stuff with my legs. I cried heaps when it finally sunk in I was never going to walk again, but Sarah helped me get over that."

Tareq looked up at Sarah, an oddly intense weighing look in his eyes, as though he was measuring her power to achieve miracles of healing.

"Sarah was the best at getting me through everything!" Jessie declared.

"Yes. I'm sure she was," he said very softly.

"Anyway, it wasn't Firefly's fault, Tareq."

His gaze dropped to Jessie again.

"It was me being dumb about the sparkler and disobeying Daddy. So you really don't have to do things for me. Besides, there's nothing to make up for," she insisted strongly, her little face determined on this point. "Walking isn't everything, you know. I can do lots. More even than I did before 'cause I think about more things."

He shook his head, bemused by the enormous strength in such a positive attitude.

Tears pricked Sarah's eyes and she fiercely blinked them back. Jessie didn't want her tears. She wanted approval like everyone else. "You certainly do," she said half-laughingly. "What you've been sending me on the computer is marvellous."

Jessie giggled happily. Her eyes actually flirted in a very female way as she addressed Tareq again. "Mind you, I won't say no if you think of more things for me, Tareq."

"Jessie..." His face had softened into an expression of almost awe...certainly the warmest admiration. "You give me more than you receive." He leaned over and softly kissed her forehead. "Thank you for telling me your story."

She glowed under his kindness. "I just didn't want you to have it wrong."

"I have it right. Perfectly right," he assured her, squeezing her hand again as he stood up. "Sleep well, my dear Jessie. I must go now, but your spirit goes with me."

Jessie was content to be left, having squared her conscience with Tareq's generosity.

As Sarah accompanied Tareq out of the suite she was aware of steely purpose emanating from him, pulsing from him. Although she was walking beside him, she felt she was walking alone. He was focused on something else, intensely focused.

Afraid it might relate to her father, she said, "I think Dad might have justified what he did...because of Firefly. Not that it's any excuse, but..."

"Your father doesn't matter, Sarah." He stopped and

spun her towards him, his hands grasping her upper arms, his face blazing with a look of enlightened and ruthless power. "From the mouth of a child... My God! Sarah! To put so much behind her and go forward as she has done...and you were there to help her. You were with her. I need no more. I will do no less."

He kissed her forehead as he had done Jessie's, then left her, taking the corridor that led to his administrative centre, every stride away from her firmly decisive.

CHAPTER NINETEEN

THE banquet room in the palace was a long way from the one at Marchington Hall, in every sense. The riches here were dazzling; a mirrored ceiling ornately latticed in gold, magnificent marble columns supporting wonderfully carved arches coated with gold leaf, fantastic friezes, a marble floor seemingly grained with gold, and the exotically designed table and chairs standing on gold legs. The chairs were upholstered in a gleaming silk imprinted with a shimmering peacock's tail pattern, and peacock feathers wavered from wonderful gold urns set around the room.

Sarah was glad she had chosen to wear the wine red dress Tareq had bought her in Paris, adding the long-sleeved bolero that had come with it, mindful of the modesty expected of women in this culture. The ruby necklace and earrings felt right tonight. She wanted Tareq to be proud of her in front of his family and certainly anything else she owned would have been hopelessly outshone by this room.

Besides, every woman here—his stepmother, half-sisters, cousins—was fabulously dressed, glowing like gloriously plumaged birds amongst the formal white robes worn by the men. She fitted into the company…more or less…though she was extremely conscious of not being family. She was the only one here who was not kin. Even Peter Larsen had been excluded from this pre-wedding gathering.

174

Sarah couldn't help wondering what it meant...Tareq putting her in the spotlight like this. He, of course, was at the head of the long table. She was seated on his right, opposite his uncle whom she had met for the first time tonight. She had half-expected to feel hostility coming from the formidable old man, yet he was showing her every courtesy, conversing with her in a respectful manner which obviously pleased Tareq.

Perhaps it was the best political move at this point, bowing to the sheikh's will. Certainly Tareq was exuding masterful authority. Sarah particularly noticed how deferential every member of his family was in addressing him or listening to what he had to say.

Had he taken some totally dominant stand with all of them or was this the normal order of things in his presence? Though what appeared on the surface need not reflect what flowed underneath, she thought soberly, remembering Penny's talk of conspiracies. All the same, in the days since Jessie's arrival, Tareq had not been quite so tense, and tonight he seemed very relaxed, happy, as though he was relieved of the burdens he'd found so testing.

The long dinner with his family proved less of an ordeal than Sarah had imagined it would be. After coffee had been served, Tareq rose from his chair to command attention, obviously intent on making a speech. Talk stopped. Heads turned to him. Sarah marvelled at the power he held, an innate charisma that simply fanned out from him, creating a magnetic field. A born leader, she thought, a man of destiny, and if that destiny could not include her, then she was still fortunate to have known his love.

A stab of pain accompanied the thought, but there was

pride, too, and when he momentarily met her gaze before beginning his speech, his vivid blue eyes burned with a fire that encompassed more than the desire to have her with him. There was a flame of exaltation, as though they had reached some glorious pinnacle together, and only with her could he stay there. It gave her a beautiful feeling, a sense of completeness, of having loved well...even if not wisely.

"For many years, our lives have travelled side by side," he started. "The sense of a family going forward is a matter of satisfaction and pride. For our family, it also carries a strong sense of responsibility to our country, an ongoing leadership that is trusted and esteemed. Our people look to us to care for them and give them a secure and stable government."

He paused to smile benevolently. "With the marriage of my brother, Ahmed, to our cousin, Aisha, the bond of unity is strengthened, and I wish them both a long, happy life and many children."

There was a smattering of applause around the table, eager murmurs of agreement trailing into silence for Tareq to continue.

"As you all know, it is the custom of our country that the firstborn son of the sheikh becomes the sheikh after him. This tradition has been practised through many generations of our family. I hold my position through right of birth, and it could be seen as my duty to marry and have a son, who would be my natural successor."

These words were not so happily received. The mood of the company subtly changed. Sarah sensed tension underneath a stirring of unrest. Several frosty glances were thrown her way. She was obviously a bone of contention, bringing disfavour on Tareq's judgment and probably raising questions over his respect for the position he had inherited.

It was a highly discomforting moment...realising that her being here was not working for Tareq, apart from the personal intimacy he still wanted. She didn't belong in this country and never would. Surely he understood that and appreciated the ramifications of flouting his people's sense of rightness.

Tareq, however did not appear perturbed by the negative vibrations coming their way. "As I am the ruling authority," he stated with arrogant disregard for any disapproval, "I have the power to change customs and law as I see fit."

More than unrest now. Grumblings, anger, open resentment at his high-handedness, glares at Sarah as though she were the instigator of the changes to come. It wasn't true, she fiercely told herself. Tareq was his own master. She was not a party to any of his decisions here.

Tareq's uncle gave him a hard, knowing look. Unbelievably, Tareq smiled at him, a whimsical, carefree little smile. It had the effect of focusing attention on him again.

"Your alarm cements the decision I have already made," he said, his confidence unshaken. Then his gaze turned to Sarah, his eyes like lasers, irresistible power boring into her, commanding her acquiescence as he held out his hand to her. "Will you stand by me, Sarah?"

Uproar.

She stared at him in disbelief. He couldn't mean to announce a marriage with her. He couldn't! He hadn't even asked her!

His uncle crashed his fist on the table, rising to his feet. "No! It cannot be done, Tareq," he growled.

"Sarah…" The repeated call to her carried unwavering purpose.

The noise around her seemed to recede into a distant wash of sound. The thunder of her heart filled her ears. Her legs trembled but she pushed up from her chair and grasped the hand held out to her, compelled beyond sense and reason to stand with him against the whole world, if that was his will.

His uncle, aggressively angry. "Tareq, I warn you…"

"Enough!" came the steely reply. A strong sweep of his arm brought the noise around the table down to a subdued mutter. "You will hear me out with the respect I am due."

His uncle sat. A mutinous silence settled. Tareq interlaced his fingers with Sarah's, gripping hard. Fear was quaking through her. Not even Tareq with his dominating will could make people accept what they didn't want to. If he was entertaining the idea of making her his consort, the journey ahead looked impossible, loaded with landmines. Yet if he wanted her with him…

"Firstly, I wish to thank you, Uncle, for your loyal support over the years, and for the important service you have given to our country on my behalf. Your advice has been invaluable and I heed it now. I also accept the truth of what you have told me."

The old man compressed his lips and shook his head.

Tareq shifted his attention to encompass his family and spoke with ringing conviction. "The ruling sheikh should give himself wholeheartedly to his people and his country, belonging to them as they belong to him. The bonds of trust and loyalty go deep. They are rooted in a shared heritage, a shared understanding, a shared life, a perception of the sheikh as being of the people and for the people he rules."

Vehement nods around the table.

"I have lived my life in two worlds," Tareq went on. "And I shall continue to do so, at the service of my country and my family."

Instant protests. Insistence that he reconsider the position he was striking.

Tareq raised his hand and silence fell again, a brooding belligerent silence.

"I am mindful of what is needed here." He paused to lend weight to his words. Scepticism hung heavily around the table. "And I know I am not the man who can best fulfil it."

Surprise, frowns at this extraordinary admission. Suspicion of trickery.

"Therefore, with the power invested in me, I now change the customary order of succession. The official announcement of my abdication will be made public tomorrow."

Shock! Total shock!

Sarah's mind buzzed with horror. If he was doing this for her... Dear Heaven! Giving up all that was rightfully his... How could she live with such a sacrifice! But there was nothing she could do or say to change his decision. The line was already drawn. He had passed the point of no return.

"Ahmed..." Tareq's gaze fastened on the man seated at the foot of the table, his oldest half-brother, the bridegroom-to-be. Every head turned to Ahmed, who stiffened, straightening in his chair, his handsome face struggling to comprehend the enormity of what was happening. "...I pass my authority to you," Tareq declared, ripping straight to the heart of the matter. "It is you who can truly wear it. You are more our father's son than I am, and I know your sense of responsibility to our people will lead you to use your authority with their best interests at heart."

Cries of approval erupted, the shock fading as all confusion over Tareq's intentions was erased. The nerve-tearing tension eased into relief. For everyone except Sarah. Her anxiety increased with a million uncertainties about the future.

Tareq smiled at his half-brother. "It is a timely wedding gift, is it not? It will give our people much to celebrate...the marriage of their new sheikh."

"Tareq..." Ahmed rose to his feet, his hands lifting, gesturing a plea for a settlement of their differences. "...I was not expecting you to...to..."

"I know you will accept this mantle with dignity, my brother, and wear it with honour. Come..." Tareq stepped aside and waved Ahmed to the place he had vacated "...take this chair. It is yours."

His head high, shoulders straight, eyes shining, Ahmed walked directly to Tareq and embraced him. The two men exchanged kisses of respect on both cheeks.

"Aisha...this chair on the right hand of your sheikh will belong to you. Come and be seated beside your betrothed."

She, too, moved with great dignity, bowing to Tareq before standing by Ahmed. Neither of them sat. They waited, they all waited for Tareq's next pronouncement.

"Uncle, I am sure you will counsel them well in their duties. As you know, their hearts are already in the right place. On mine there is another claim."

He recaptured Sarah's hand, enfolding it now in comforting warmth. He raised his other hand in a salute of farewell. "I leave you to welcome and celebrate our new regime. I wish you all a very good night."

Chairs instantly scraped back. Everyone stood in respect as Tareq and Sarah made their unified exit from the banquet room. Only the sound of their footsteps on the marble floor accompanied them out, and to Sarah, they seemed to echo in a great emptiness. Tareq had cut himself off from a world that had occupied half his life. Probably more than half. How was the hole to be filled?

CHAPTER TWENTY

FREE…elation zinged through Tareq…free of the duality that had plagued him since early boyhood, free to take new paths, free to keep the companion of his heart, free to choose how to live, where to live, and with whom to live.

Maybe this was the high before the low of feeling the loss of all the privileges attached to his former status, but he doubted they were worth caring about. Jessie had it right. When one power was irretrievably gone, the incentive to find and use others pushed useless regrets into the discard bin. Besides, over and above everything else was the love he couldn't bear to lose.

It was colour.

It was meaning.

It gave him the sense of belonging he had always craved and never known…before Sarah.

Happiness surged through him as he closed his door to the rest of the palace, ensuring their absolute and intimate privacy in his apartment. His blood was singing. His soul was soaring. His eyes feasted on the woman who had braved a journey of faith with him, matching him every step of the way, despite the risks, the tests of strength, the trials and tribulations thrust upon her by the demands of who he was and what was expected of him.

No more.

The way ahead was clear now if she would share it with him.

He tore off his headdress and tossed it onto a chair. There was only one thing left to do and he whirled Sarah into his embrace, buoyantly confident of the outcome he wanted. Her hands fluttered against his chest, signalling her inner agitation.

"You think I've given up too much," he said, reading the distress and worry in her eyes.

"Tareq, you once told me love always had a price. But this…" She shook her head in anguish. "It's impossible for me to count all you've sacrificed."

"It's not a sacrifice. It's a gain, my darling." He gently smoothed the lines from her forehead. "Have you ever wondered what your life was about? What it was for?"

Her eyes remained anxious.

"I was brainwashed from childhood to accept and fulfil a role I didn't choose," he explained. "There were times I railed against it. My English half rebelled. I felt burdened with duties I was not in tune with. Yet my responsibilities did give my life purpose, and with the power I had, I could make things happen. Both factors influenced my view of what was worthwhile. Everything, I thought, was relative to that central core of purpose to achieve for my country."

"Then won't you feel a terrible gap in a future that doesn't hold that?" she fretted.

"It holds something different. Something more worthwhile to me," he replied with passionate conviction.

She trembled. "How do you know?"

"Because any purpose pales in comparison to what you give me. Your gift of love is beyond price."

Tears put a luminous sheen on the conflict still evident in her eyes. She swallowed, determined on voicing her doubts. "Tareq, you're used to having more than me in your life."

"So? I still have more. Sarah, my love, I have a vast, personal fortune. I can play with whatever market offers me a satisfying challenge. We can do it together...publishing...breeding dogs and horses..." He laughed. "The sky is the limit and the world is ours. *There's* the difference, Sarah. It will be *our* world, not one imposed on us. And we get to say who belongs in it."

She looked at him searchingly. "You're really happy about this?"

"Oh, yes. You see before you a man no longer divided." He smiled reassuringly. "However, I would like one guarantee on the future."

"Tareq, there aren't any guarantees. You may regret..."

He touched his fingertips to her lips, cutting off any looking back. A new life had begun. "I won't regret anything if you will give me one promise and keep it."

"What is it?"

He moved his hand to cup her cheek, tenderly, persuasively, possessively. "Say you will marry me."

Still the anxious caring for him, yet overlaid by a growing look of awe, of wonder. "You trust me that much?' she asked huskily, a deep well of emotion furring her voice.

"It's not trust, Sarah. It's love."

Tears hovered on her lashes. Her mouth quivered. Tareq felt his heart turn over. She was so beautiful. So vulnerable. The desire to love her, protect her, give her everything she needed and wanted, streamed through him, finding no barrier, no trace of conflict, not even a pause for second thought.

He kissed her, softly, tenderly, longingly. "Say yes, Sarah. Say yes," he urged, needing to hear it, knowing he wouldn't feel complete without her verbal commitment.

"Yes," she whispered.

Her mouth said it. Her body said it. There was no holding back. None at all. And he held nothing back. He didn't have to. They were truly one.

The foundation for their future was set, their journey together assured. It was much later that night, lying in contentment with Sarah nestled close to him, Tareq remembered the day she'd walked back into his life, and the answer he'd given her when she'd asked how long their journey was to be.

Until I know it all.

He smiled.

He'd spoken a truth not encompassed by the arrogant confidence he'd felt at the time. Impossible to know it all, even given a lifetime. He was only at the beginning of unlocking his mind and unfolding his heart to the love Sarah had brought to him. He looked ahead to the many pleasures of having her as his wife...the children they would have together...the family they would create and bond in an unbreakable sense of belonging...it was endless, their journey.

Endless.

And he loved the thought of every minute of it.

CHAPTER TWENTY-ONE

"FIREFLY sitting eighth, well positioned in the field as they come around the bend…"

Eighth…it was where he had finished in the Melbourne Cup last year. Sarah's heart was pounding as hard as the horses' hooves hitting the turf. Firefly had to do better. He had to. She desperately wanted the exonerating proof that her father was doing his best by Tareq's horses.

She was sure he was…the whole family was here to watch the big race, the twins madly excited, Susan smilingly confident, Jessie glowing with pleasure, her father eager to discuss anything and everything with Tareq. Nevertheless, only a really good performance would take away the stigma of shoddy training.

"Come on, Firefly!" Jessie yelled. Peter Larsen had hoisted her up against his shoulder to give her a clear view and she was jiggling wildly, making Peter laugh.

He was really a very nice man underneath his rather austere exterior, and still Tareq's trouble-shooter, though there was less trouble to deal with these days. Sarah wondered if the crooked bookmaker was here at Flemington and swiftly squashed the awful thought. It had nothing to do with them anymore.

"Into the straight with four hundred metres to go and Firefly is making a move…"

Was it too soon? Could he stay the distance if he went

to the front now? Doubts and fears swirled through Sarah's mind. If he flagged before the winning post...

"Come on, Firefly!" Jessie yelled, and the twins yelled to see, too.

Tareq scooped them up against his shoulders. Sarah couldn't help smiling. He was going to make a wonderful father. She touched her slightly rounded stomach. Thank heaven the morning sickness was over. She was churning enough as it was without that added nausea.

The whole crowd was yelling now. The field of horses was bunching up, the jockeys urging their mounts into a final sprint.

"Two hundred metres to go and Firefly takes the lead..."

He looked magnificent, powering ahead at full stretch, a long neck in front, then half a length, a full length... Sarah tore her gaze away from the race to look at her father. Was it all right? Could Firefly maintain this speed?

Her father caught her anxious glance and winked reassuringly. "He's a champion stayer," he said with pride.

The children were cheering him on, beside themselves with excitement. Sarah heard herself screaming, "Yes...yes...go!" as the distance to cover grew less and less and still Firefly held his lead. It was impossible, she thought, but miracles did happen. Wasn't she married to Tareq? With their very own family on the way? And she was even friends with her mother now!

The winning post was coming up...two other horses on his heels, gaining on him bit by bit, but surely Firefly would have to falter for them to catch and pass him.

And he didn't. He just kept flying, poetry in motion, and they were all screaming, even Tareq.

"And it's Firefly, the winner of this year's Melbourne Cup…"

Sarah burst into tears. Her father wrapped her in a bear hug and rocked her with his own glee. "Your old Dad wouldn't be letting you down when you're about to make him a Grandpa, now would he?" he chortled. "I'll be taking Firefly to win the Japan Cup next."

"And well you might, Drew," Tareq declared, clapping him on the back in delighted approval.

It was wonderful. Everyone was deliriously happy. A horserace shouldn't mean so much, Sarah thought, but today it did. Today, with Firefly actually winning, felt like the crowning glory of the year in her life when everything had come right for her and all the promises had been kept.

As they were going down to the winner's enclosure for the presentation of the cup, she stumbled on the stairs. Even as Tareq caught her to him, Peter, two steps ahead, whirled to save her from falling. He breathed a sigh of relief as he saw she was safe.

"That's my godchild you're carrying," he archly reminded her.

She smiled. "Don't worry, Peter. You'll have plenty of chances. We're planning on half a dozen children at least."

He raised an eyebrow. "Brave words."

"And trouble," she laughed at him.

He grinned. "I've never minded good trouble."

"Well, we can guarantee you plenty of that," Tareq informed him, as high-spirited as the rest of them.

The whole family gathered around the dais where the

official presentation was to be made. Firefly was there, too, being paraded in front of the crowd. Speeches flowed. Tareq, as the owner of the winning horse, should have had the cup presented to him, but he insisted it be given to his wife. After all, it wouldn't have been won without her, he argued. She was the miracle in his life. And always would be.

Sarah didn't have a speech prepared. She looked at her father and his family, so proud and happy and secure in their togetherness. She looked at Peter and thought of trust and loyalty and caring. She looked at Tareq and saw the love in his eyes...her husband, her partner in the journey of life...and the words came from her heart.

"This cup represents a dream fulfilled..."